Enid Blyton

The
Amelia Jane
Collection

EGMONT

We bring stories to life

Naughty Amelia Jane! first published in Great Britain in 1946 by Newnes
Amelia Jane Again! first published in Great Britain in 1946 by Newnes
Amelia Jane is Naughty Again! first published in Great Britain in 1954 by Newnes

This edition first published in Great Britain in 2007 by Dean,
an imprint of Egmont UK Limited, 239 Kensington High Street,
London W8 6SA

ISBN 978 0 6035 6356 0

5 7 9 10 8 6

Printed and bound in Spain

CONTENTS

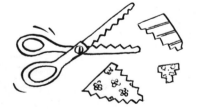

BOOK ONE

Naughty Amelia Jane!

Contents

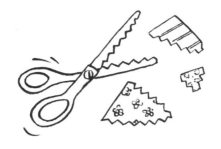

Naughty Amelia Jane

The toys in the nursery were very friendly with the small pixies who lived in the bushes below the nursery window. The pixies had no wings, but they managed to climb up the tall pear tree and get in at the window whenever it was open. So you can guess that the toys and the pixies had many a good game!

There was one very naughty toy, who often made the others really angry. This was Amelia Jane, a big, long-legged doll with an ugly face, a bright red frock, and yellow hair. She hadn't come from a shop, like the others, but had been made at home. Shop-toys nearly always have good manners, and know how to behave themselves – but Amelia Jane, not being a shop-toy, had no manners at all, and didn't care what she said or did!

Once she poured a jug of milk down Tom the toy soldier's neck, and that made him wet and uncomfortable for two days. Another time she threw a woollen ball up so

high that it went into the goldfish
globe, and made the poor goldfish
jump almost out of his skin. Then,
when the teddy bear climbed up to get
the ball out of the water, Amelia Jane

climbed up behind him, gave him a push – and there was the poor bear, spluttering away in the water, and trying his hardest to swim, whilst the goldfish darted at him in fury.

Dear dear, how Amelia Jane laughed, and how all the other toys shouted at her! Whatever would she do next?

The next thing she did was to catch a bee in a matchbox, and then, when the sailor doll needed matches, she gave him the matchbox, pretending that there were matches inside. You can imagine how scared

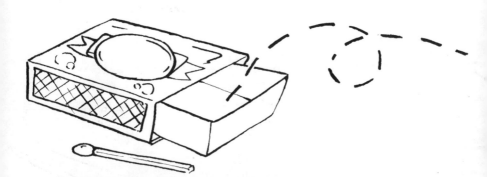

he was when a bee flew out and stung
him on the nose!

'Amelia Jane, you are a perfect
nuisance,' said the toys angrily.
'Can't you settle down and be good
like us? One day you will do
something that will get us all into
trouble!'

'Pooh!' said Amelia Jane rudely.
'I shan't!'

But she did do
something very

naughty indeed the next time.

She was hunting about in Nanny's work-basket for a thimble to play with, when she came across Nanny's scissors. Ho! Now she could have a fine game of cutting!

So she took the scissors and began to snip-snip-snip everything! The other toys were sitting in a corner playing a game of snap, and they didn't notice at first what Amelia Jane was doing. They wouldn't let Amelia play snap with them because she said 'Snap!' when it wasn't, and took away all their cards.

So Amelia Jane had a lovely time all by herself. She snipped a hole in the curtains, and then she snipped

another! Then she went to the hearth-
rug and cut a whole corner off that!
Then she found Nanny's handkerchief
on the floor, and do you know, she cut
it into twenty-two tiny pieces! It was
one of Nanny's best hankies too, with
a pretty lace edge. But Amelia Jane
didn't care about that!

Then she went to the carpet and

began to snip little bits of it here and there. The carpet was a green one with red roses, and wherever Amelia could see a rose, she snipped! Wasn't it dreadful of her?

The toys took no notice. They were having such a lovely game. Amelia grew cross with them for being happy without her. So what do you suppose she did? She went up behind the pink rabbit and snipped his tail off!

Goodness! You should have seen how he jumped!

'Ooooooooh!' he yelled. 'She's snipped my tail off! Look! Oh, the wicked, wicked doll!'

'And look what else she's done!'

cried the toys in horror, pointing to the spoilt hanky, the snipped rug, and the cut carpet. 'And look, she's spoilt the curtains too. Oh, what trouble we shall get into! Nanny will know it must be the toys, and she will throw us all into the dustbin! Oh!'

The toys stared in horror at all that the naughty doll had done. The pink rabbit cried bitterly, for he felt dreadful without a tail. Oh dear! How he would be laughed at, now that he hadn't a tail! Tom the toy soldier put his arm round him and comforted him.

'Don't worry, Bunny,' he said. 'We shall all love you just the same, even if you don't wear a tail, and look rather like a guinea-pig!'

The pink rabbit cried all the more loudly when he heard that. 'I don't want to be like a guinea-pig!' he wept. 'I want to be like a rabbit! I hate Amelia Jane! Punish her, Tom! She is a very wicked doll!'

Amelia Jane laughed. She loved doing naughty things. She liked seeing all the toys staring in horror at the mischief she had done. Ha, Ha! That would teach them to play snap without her!

'Give me those scissors,' said Tom sternly.

'Shan't!' said Amelia Jane, twirling them round in her big hand.

'I said, "Give me those scissors!" '

ordered the toy soldier.

'I said "Shan't!" ' said Amelia
Jane, 'and if you talk to me like that,
Tom, I'll chop your hat into little
pieces! Then you'll look horrid!'

'You naughty, wicked doll!' said
Tom, in a fury. But he didn't dare to
try to take the scissors away, for they
had very sharp points, and he really
was afraid that Amelia Jane would cut
up his lovely hat. He was very proud
of it, and he didn't want anything to
happen to it.

'Whatever shall we do?' said the
teddy bear. The toys all looked at one
another in despair.

Then they heard a little scraping
noise at the window, and they saw

their friends, the pixies, creeping in at the crack at the bottom.

'Hallo, Toys! You look very miserable!' said the pixies, scrambling down from the window-seat to the floor. 'What's the matter? Have you lost a pound and found a penny?'

'No,' said the toys. 'Just look here, pixies, at what Amelia Jane has done!'

'I say!' said the pixies, staring at all the damage. 'Why did you let her have scissors? And look, she still has them. You ought to take them away from her before she does any more mischief.'

'She won't let us have them,' said Tom. 'She says she will chop my hat into little pieces if I try to take them from her.'

'Oho, we'll soon see to that!' said
the biggest pixie at once. 'Scissors,
come to me!'

He waved his little gold wand –
and immediately the scissors flew out
of Amelia Jane's hand and went to the
pixie. He caught them and gave them
to Tom.

'Oh, thank you,' said the toys
gratefully. 'I suppose you couldn't
help us to mend all these dreadful
holes and slits that Amelia has made?'

'Oh yes, I think so,' said the
biggest pixie. 'We'll just go and get
our needles and thread, and come
back to help you. We'll sew everything
so that you won't see even a tiny

stitch! We are very clever at stitching, you know. Once we sewed all the petals on a daisy that had lost hers in a rainstorm – and you really couldn't see that they were not growing! As for that handkerchief, we'll use a bit of magic for that, and all the bits will join together so that Nanny will never know it has been cut!'

The pixies fetched their needles and thread, and soon they were sitting on the carpet and on the rug, mending all the slits and cuts, and two of them mended the curtains. Then the biggest pixie put a spell into his needle and sewed on the bunny's tail again. It didn't hurt a bit because of the spell. The bunny was so grateful.

The handkerchief was mended too –
and everything was put right.

'There!' said the pixies, in delight.
'We've done all we can!'

'We can't thank you enough!' said
the toys. 'You may be sure that if ever
we can help you in return we will!'

'As for Amelia Jane,' said the biggest
pixie, 'I should keep her a prisoner in
the toy-cupboard until she says she is
sorry and won't be naughty any more.
Here is a spell that will keep her there!'

Tom took the spell. It was in a little
box, and when it was taken out and
blown over Amelia, she had to stay
where she was put. The toys
surrounded the naughty doll, pushed

her into the cupboard, and then blew the spell at her. She couldn't move her legs! There she had to stay!

At first she was very angry. Then she was frightened, and begged to be set free. She saw the toys going happily about their play, and she wanted to join them. It was dreadfully dull in the toy-cupboard all alone except for a box of bricks that never said a word.

'I'm sorry, Toys! Do set me free!' begged Amelia Jane. 'I will try very hard not to be naughty any more.'

'If we could be sure you would do good things and not naughty ones, *we would* set you free,' said Tom. 'But we don't trust you. You have never done a good or brave thing all the time you have been with us.'

Amelia Jane was just going to answer him when there came a tapping at the window. The toys looked up. A small red robin was there. He looked most excited.

'What is it?' shouted the toys, swarming up to the window-seat.

'It's the pixies!' said the robin. 'They have been attacked by the goblins! They have hidden in the old hollow tree, but the goblins are cutting it down! Can you rescue them?'

'How?' said Tom, upset and bothered to hear such bad news.

'I don't know,' said the robin. 'You'll have to think of something – but hurry, because at any moment the goblins may get them!'

He flew off, and the toys crowded together, all talking at once.

'Toys, Toys, I have a plan!' cried Amelia Jane from the cupboard. 'Let me fly the toy aeroplane out of the window. It will frighten the goblins terribly, and they are sure to run away. Then, before they come back, the pixies can get into the aeroplane and I'll fly it safely back here!'

'All right!' shouted the toys, excited. 'It's a good idea. Set her free, Tom.'

So Amelia Jane was set free. The aeroplane was run up to her, and she got in. Rr-rr-rr-rr-rr! It shot up into the air and out of the window. How exciting it was! Amelia was a bit afraid of falling out, but she managed to guide the aeroplane to the hollow tree. Then down she flew – and all the little goblins who were cutting down the tree to get at the pixies inside, cried out in horror:

'Run! Run! The aeroplane is coming down on top of us!'

They scattered in fright. Amelia
stopped the aeroplane and landed by
the hollow tree. She called to the
pixies:

'Pixies! Quickly! Get into my
aeroplane! I've come to rescue you!'

The pixies all shot out of the
hollow tree at once and clambered
into the plane. When the goblins saw
what was happening they gave a
shout of rage and ran to the
aeroplane at once – but it was too
late. Rr-rr-rr-rr-rr! It rose into the air,
and flew straight back to the nursery
window. In two minutes the pixies
were safe in the nursery with the toys,
and *how* pleased they were!

'Amelia Jane has turned over a

new leaf,' said the pixies, in surprise. 'Brave Amelia Jane! Thank you so much for rescuing us!'

'Don't mention it!' said Amelia. 'I am trying very hard to be good now.'

And you will be pleased to hear that she certainly *was* good for a little while, but I'm afraid it didn't last for very long!

Amelia Jane Gets a Shock

Well, for a little while Amelia Jane was very good – and then, oh dear, she forgot all her promises, and became really naughty! The things she did!

She took a needle and cotton out of Nanny's work-basket, and sewed up the sleeves of the teddy bear's new coat when he wasn't looking. So when he went to put on his coat, he simply could *not* put his arms through the sleeves anyhow! He just couldn't find the way in – because the sleeves were sewn up! How Amelia Jane laughed to see him!

The next night she hid behind the curtain and began to mew like a cat. The toys were not very fond of Tibs the cat, because he sometimes chewed them. So they all stopped playing and looked round to see where Tibs was.

'I can hear him mewing!' said the teddy bear. 'He must be behind the door.'

But he wasn't. Amelia mewed

again. The toys hunted all about for the cat. They even looked in the coal-scuttle, and under the hearth-rug, which made Amelia laugh till she nearly choked! She mewed again, very loudly.

'Where is that cat!' cried Tom the toy soldier, in despair. 'We've looked everywhere! Is he behind the curtain?'

'No, there's only Amelia Jane there!' said the golden-haired doll, looking. 'There's no cat.'

Well, of course, they didn't find any cat at all! And Amelia Jane didn't tell them it was she who had been mewing, so to this day they wonder where Tibs hid himself that night!

Then Amelia Jane saw a soda-water siphon left in a corner of the room. She knew how it worked, because she had seen Nanny using one. Oh, what fun it would be to squirt all the toys! She stole towards it – picked it up, and dear me, it *was* heavy! She ran at the surprised Tom, pressed down the handle – and out gushed the soda-water all over him!

'Ow! Ooh!' he shouted, in astonishment. 'What is it? What is it? Amelia Jane, you ought to be ashamed of yourself!'

But she wasn't a bit ashamed. She was just enjoying herself thoroughly! She ran after the teddy bear and soaked him with soda-water too. She squirted lots over the clockwork mouse, and made him so wet that for two days his clockwork went wrong, and he couldn't be wound up. She squirted the pink rabbit, and he got into the wastepaper basket and couldn't get out, which worried him very much, because he was so afraid that Jane, the cleaner, would throw him away the next day! But she didn't, which was very lucky.

'Amelia Jane is up to her tricks again,' said the clockwork clown, frowning. 'We shall have no peace at all. What shall we do?'

'Take away her key!' said the clockwork mouse.

'She hasn't one, silly!' said Tom.

'Lock her in the cupboard!' said the teddy bear.

'She knows how to undo it from the inside,' said the pink rabbit gloomily.

Nobody spoke for a whole minute. They were all thinking hard.

Then the clockwork clown gave a little laugh. 'I know!' he said. 'I've thought of an idea. It's quite simple, but it might work.'

'What?' cried everyone.

'Let's polish Amelia Jane's shoes underneath and make them very, very slippery,' said the clown. 'Then, if she begins to run after us with soda-water siphons or things like that, down she'll go!'

'But she won't like that,' said the golden-haired doll, who was rather tender-hearted.

'Well, *we* don't like the tricks she plays on *us*!' said Tom. 'We'll do it, Clown! When she next takes her shoes off we'll polish them underneath till they are as slippery as glass!'

The very next night Amelia Jane took off her shoes because she said her feet were hot. She put the shoes into a corner and then danced round the nursery in her stockinged feet, enjoying herself. The clown picked up the shoes and ran away to the back of the toy-cupboard with them. He had a tiny duster there, and a little bit of polish he had taken out of Jane's polish jar when the nursery had been cleaned out. Aha, Amelia Jane, you'll be sorry for all your tricks!

The clown polished and rubbed, rubbed and polished. The soles of the shoes shone. They were as slippery as could be! The clown put them back and waited for Amelia Jane to put them on. This she very soon did, for she had stepped on a pin and pricked her foot! As she put her shoes on, she thought out a naughty trick!

I'll run after all the toys with that pin I trod on! she thought. Oooh! That will make them rush away into all the corners! What fun it will be to frighten them!

She buttoned her shoes and took the nasty long pin into her hand. Then she stood up and looked round, her naughty eyes gleaming.

I'll run after that fat little teddy bear! she thought. So off she went, straight at the teddy holding the pin out in front of her.

'Amelia Jane, put that pin down!' shouted the teddy bear in fright – but before Amelia Jane had taken three steps, her very, very slippery shoes slid along the ground and down she fell, bumpity-bump! She *was* so surprised!

Up she got again and took a few more steps towards the teddy bear – but her shoes slipped and down she fell! Bumpity-bump! She hit her head on the fender!

'What's the matter with the carpet?' cried Amelia Jane in a rage. 'It keeps making me fall down!'

'Ha ha! ho ho!' laughed the toys. 'Perhaps there is slippery magic about, Amelia Jane!'

'Oh, I believe you toys have something to do with it!' shouted the angry doll. Up she got and took the pin in her hand again. 'I'll show you what happens to people who put slippery magic on the floor! Here comes my pin!'

She tried to run at Tom, who was laughing so much that the tears ran all down his face. But down she went again, bumpity-bump – and oh my, the pin stuck into her knee! Yes, it really did – she fell on it!

How Amelia Jane squealed! How Amelia Jane wept! 'Oh, the horrid pin! Oh, how it hurts!' she cried.

'Well, Amelia Jane, it serves you right,' said the pink rabbit. 'You were going to prick *us* with that pin and now it's pricked *you*! You know how it feels!'

Amelia Jane threw the pin away in a rage. The clown picked it up and flung it into the fire! He wasn't going to have pins about the nursery!

Amelia Jane got up again. 'I'm going to bandage my knee where the pin pricked it,' she said. She ran to the toy cupboard – but before she was halfway there, her slippery shoes slid away beneath her – and down she sat with a dreadful bumpity-bumpity-bump!

The toys laughed. Amelia Jane cried bitterly. The golden-haired doll felt sorry for her. 'Don't cry any more, Amelia Jane,' she said. 'Take your shoes off and you won't fall again. We played a trick on you – but you can't complain because you have so often tricked *us*! You should not play jokes on other people if you can't take a joke yourself!'

Amelia Jane took her shoes off. She saw how the clown had polished them underneath, and she went very red. She knew quite well she could not grumble if people were unkind – because she too had been unkind.

'I'll try and be good, Toys,' she said at last. 'It's difficult for me, because I'm not a shop-toy like you, so I haven't learnt good manners and nice ways. But I may be good one day!'

The toys thought it was nice of her to say all that. The golden-haired doll came to help her bandage her knee. The clown put a bandage round her head where she had bumped it. She looked so funny that they didn't know

whether to laugh or cry at her.

Amelia Jane did enjoy being fussed! She was as nice as could be to the toys – but oh dear, oh dear, I do somehow feel perfectly certain that she can't be good for long!

Amelia Jane at the Sea

Once it happened that Amelia Jane, the big, naughty doll, was taken down to the seaside with some of the other toys. The clockwork clown went, the brown teddy bear, Tom the toy soldier, and the golden-haired doll. They went in the car with the children, and they were all most excited.

'I shall dig in the sand and throw it

over everybody!' said naughty Amelia Jane. 'And I shall get my pail and fill it full of water and pour it down Tom's neck! Ho, won't he jump!'

'You'll do nothing of the sort, Amelia Jane,' said Tom at once. 'You know how often you've promised to be good. Well, just you remember your promise.'

'And I shall push the clockwork clown into a rock-pool and make him sit down there with all his clothes on,' said Amelia Jane, with a naughty giggle.

'You mustn't!' cried the clown, in alarm. 'If you do that, my clockwork will get rusty and I shan't wind up properly – then I won't be able to walk any more, or turn head-over-heels!'

The children often took the toys down to the beach with them. After dinner the children went to have a rest, and the toys were left in a sheltered corner of the beach. No one ever came there, so the children knew they were quite safe. And it was whilst the toys were left alone there that Amelia Jane behaved so very badly. She did all she said she would, and more too.

She threw sand all over the golden-haired doll, and it went into her eyes dreadfully. She cried, and Tom had to find his handkerchief and comfort her. Whilst he was patting the doll on the back, and wiping the sand out of her eyes, Amelia Jane was filling her pail from a pool.

She crept up behind Tom and tipped the pail of cold sea-water all down his neck!

'Ooooo-ow-oooo!' yelled Tom, jumping about twelve centimetres into the air with fright. 'You wicked doll, Amelia Jane! I told you not to do that!'

Amelia Jane thought it was such a funny joke that she rolled over and over on the sand, laughing. The clockwork clown, who had seen all that had happened, remembered what she had said she would do to him, and he ran away to hide. He really was dreadfully afraid Amelia Jane would push him into a pool. Amelia looked for him. He had hidden himself under a clump of seaweed, so she couldn't see him – but she saw the brown teddy bear!

He was walking round the edge of a deep pool, looking at the crabs there. Amelia Jane crept up behind him. She gave him a push – SPLASH! The teddy landed in the pool and sat right down in the water.

'Oooooo-ow-ooooo!' he gasped, his mouth full of salty water. Amelia Jane laughed till the tears ran down her face.

'You are very naughty and unkind,' said the clockwork clown, poking his head out of the seaweed nearby. 'You are a most dreadful doll. Hi, Tom, come and help me push Amelia Jane into the water!'

'I shan't let you!' said Amelia Jane, at once. 'I shall paddle out to sea and sit on that rock over there. I am bigger than any of you, and I can get through the deep water easily. You won't be able to follow me. I shall be quite safe. Ha ha to you, clockwork clown!'

Amelia Jane had no shoes or socks on. She lifted up her red skirt and stepped into the waves. She waded out towards the big, big rock that showed itself some way out. It was covered with green seaweed. The teddy shook the water from his fur and ran after Amelia, splashing through the waves. But he was afraid of getting drowned, and he soon came back. Amelia was a very big doll, so she could easily get to the rock. The water did not come to more than her knees.

She reached the rock and climbed up. She waved to the others.

'I'm the king of the castle!' she
shouted, dancing on the rock. 'You
can't get me! I shall stay here and
have a nice nap!'

She lay down on the soft green
seaweed. The hot sun had dried it
well. It was like a soft bed.

Amelia fell asleep. When the
children came out to play, they didn't
miss her. They had new spades and
they wanted to dig a big castle.

They took no notice of any of the
other toys, and didn't even see how
wet the teddy bear was. They dug
and dug and dug.

They had tea on the beach and
then they dug again. When it was
time to go home they collected their

toys and set off up the beach. They had the clockwork clown, the bear, the toy soldier and the golden-haired doll – but they didn't have Amelia Jane. They had forgotten all about her.

And what about Amelia Jane? She was still asleep on the rock! The tide was now coming in – and it crept higher and higher over the rock. Soon it would reach Amelia's toes. Soon a big wave would break right over the rock on top of Amelia – and then what would happen to her?

Amelia woke up. She sat up on the rock and looked round. When she saw how the tide was coming in, she was in a dreadful fright. The water was too deep to paddle through now. She couldn't swim. Oh dear!

Amelia Jane stood and yelled for help. 'Save me, somebody!' she cried. 'Save me!' But there was no one to save her. Poor Amelia Jane!

The other toys were sitting on a shelf, watching the children go to bed. Nobody thought of Amelia Jane. They were only too glad to forget her.

But when the children were safely in bed, Tom the toy soldier suddenly looked round – and saw no Amelia. For a moment he wondered where she was – and then he remembered! She had been left on the rock – and the tide was coming in. Oooooo!

'I say, Toys,' said Tom, 'Amelia Jane's on the rock – and the sea will soon cover it right over!'

Now you might think that the clown, the golden-haired doll, and Tom would say, 'And serve Amelia right!' – but they didn't. They all looked at one another in alarm. Amelia was naughty – and she had played tricks on them – but they could not let anything horrid happen to her.

'What can we do?' asked the clown. He got down from the shelf and ran to the window. From there he could quite well see the rock on which Amelia stood, shouting for help.

'We must save her!' said the golden-haired doll.

'But how?' asked Tom.

'I know!' said the clown suddenly.

'We will take the children's toy ship – and sail it to the rock. We shall just get there in time. Hurry!'

The toy soldier and the clown caught hold of the toy ship, which lay on the floor. They ran out of the door with the golden-haired doll, and tore down to the beach. They put the boat into the water.

Tom got in. The golden-haired doll got in. The clockwork clown pushed off, and then jumped in himself. Tom arranged the white sails so that the wind filled them. The clown took the rudder and guided the little ship.

The tide was coming in fast. It was a long, long way now to the rock.

Amelia Jane was very frightened. A big wave had washed right over the rock and had wetted her to the waist. Amelia was afraid that the next one would wash her right off the rock into the big sea.

'Help! Help!' she shouted, as another big wave came over the rock. Amelia held on to some seaweed. The sea wetted her right up to her shoulders. Oooh! It was so cold! She knew now how cold Tom must have felt when she poured water down his neck that morning!

'We're coming, Amelia Jane; we're coming!' shouted the toys. Amelia Jane heard them.

She looked over the waves and saw

 the three toys in the sailing-ship. It bobbed up and down as it came, for the sea was quite rough.

'Oh, you good creatures!' sobbed Amelia Jane. 'I don't deserve to be rescued – I was so unkind to you – but oh, I'm *so* glad to see you!'

The ship sailed quite near to the rock. The clown was careful not to let it strike the rock – for that would mean a wreck. 'Jump, Amelia, jump into the ship!' he called. 'We can't come any nearer!'

Amelia Jane jumped. It was a good jump. She landed right in the middle of the boat. It swayed about, and then as the clown turned it into the wind, the sails filled and the little ship sailed towards the shore again.

'You'll soon be safe home,' said the golden-haired doll kindly. 'Don't cry, Amelia Jane.'

'I won't tease you any more, any of you,' wept Amelia. 'It was so kind of you to remember I was on the rock and come to rescue me. Thank you ever and ever so much.'

The ship reached the sand. Tom jumped out and pulled it in. The golden-haired doll jumped out and helped poor, wet, cold Amelia Jane out. The clown jumped out last of all – and then they carried the ship back to the nursery again.

Tom took Amelia Jane down to the kitchen fire and dried her. Then back to the nursery they went, and soon fell asleep after their exciting day.

And was Amelia Jane kinder to the toys after that? Yes, very much kinder, all the time they were away at the sea. But alas! When they went back home again, Amelia Jane forgot all her good ways. Read on and you will see!

Amelia Jane and the Cowboy Doll

Now one day a funny little doll came to stay with the toys in the nursery. He was a cowboy doll. He didn't belong to the children who owned the nursery, he was just lent to them for a few days.

He was dressed in shaggy trousers, leather tunic, and a cowboy hat. He was very smart indeed, and the other toys were a bit afraid of him.

He could ride the old wooden
horse, and made it gallop as fast as
could be round and round the
nursery! Once he even climbed up on
to the big rocking-horse and made it
rock so fast that the horse hrrumphed
in surprise, and Nanny came running

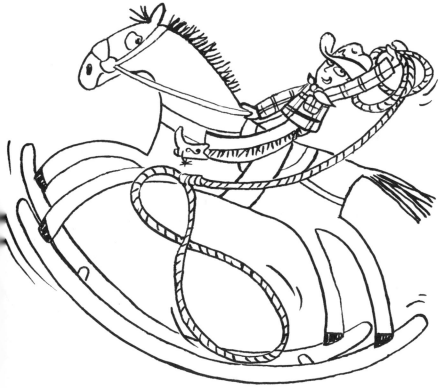

in to see what all the noise was about!

The cowboy doll only just had time to hop off the horse and lie down on the floor, where he had been put by the children!

Another thing he could do was rather marvellous. He had a long rope, and he could lasso anything with it that he liked! The toys would say to him, 'Lasso that tree on the toy farm, Cowboy doll!' And he would quickly throw his looped rope, and the end would neatly curl round the tree and topple it over!

He would lasso anything, even a pin stuck in the floor. And then, of course, Amelia Jane began to tell him naughty things to do!

'Cowboy doll, do lasso the clockwork mouse!' she whispered. 'Oh do! Look, he is over there, sniffing at that brick!'

The cowboy doll grinned. He had a most wicked face. He threw his rope neatly, and the loop at the end dropped right over the mouse's head – click!

The mouse gave a squeak of surprise and tried to run away, but the rope held him tight! He was very frightened.

'You shouldn't tell the cowboy doll to do that, Amelia Jane,' said Tom crossly. 'Why *must* you always get into mischief? Go and untie the mouse, quickly.'

'You go, Tom,' said Amelia Jane, giggling as she thought of more mischief. 'You are better at knots than I am!'

Well, the mouse was squealing so loudly that Tom really thought he had better go and help. So off he went, and Amelia Jane nudged the cowboy doll and whispered to him:

'Where's your other rope? Lasso Tom! He will get such a shock!'

So when Tom was bending over the mouse, trying to undo the loop of rope round him, there came a whizzing noise through the air, and another rope fell neatly right round Tom's waist – click! It pinned his arms to his sides and he couldn't move!

What a shock he got!

'You're my prisoner, Tom!' grinned the cowboy doll. 'Come over here!'

'I won't!' scowled Tom. 'Let me go!'

But he had to walk over to the cowboy doll and Amelia Jane because the cowboy pulled hard at the rope, and Tom had to come with it! He was so angry!

Amelia Jane thought lassoing was a lovely thing to do. She wanted to learn, and the cowboy doll said he would teach her.

'No, you are not to teach her,' said the golden-haired doll sharply. 'She is quite naughty enough without learning any more tricks. You are

NOT to teach her!'

But the cowboy doll was not used to obeying other people, so he took no notice at all. He began to teach Amelia Jane, and she tried very hard to learn.

Soon she could throw a rope wonderfully well, and then, what a time the poor toys had! They never knew when a rope was going to come whizzing through the air after them, falling over their heads and shoulders! It was most worrying.

Amelia Jane practised hard, but

she could not get quite so good at it as the cowboy doll.

Once she sent the rope flying through the air to catch the teddy bear as he walked along, and she missed him and got the rope round the chimney of the dolls' house.

Of course, she pulled too hard, and the chimney came off and fell on top of the bear's head. He was very cross indeed, and threw the chimney at

Amelia Jane. She threw it back, and it almost hit the nursery cat on the nose. He was most surprised, and looked as if he would eat Amelia Jane. So she ran into the cupboard till the cat had gone down to the kitchen for his dinner.

The toys made her climb up to the dolls' house roof and put the chimney on again. She didn't like that at all, but she had to do it. But even then she wouldn't stop lassoing things.

She lassoed the humming-top when it was spinning and made it fall down in a fright. She threw her rope at a cow in the farmyard, but caught the farmer himself and jerked him so high in the air that he really thought he was flying. He came down in the coal-scuttle and was very angry about it. He told all his cows to go and bite Amelia Jane, and she had to climb up on to a shelf out of their way.

Another time she was very naughty indeed. She thought she would lasso Mister Noah, who lived in the wooden ark, and give him a shock. He didn't like Amelia Jane, and wouldn't even say good morning to her when he met her. So Amelia waited for him to come out with all his animals.

'I'll lasso him now!' she whispered to the cowboy doll, with a grin. 'Watch me!'

She sent the rope through the air – whizz! But she missed Mister Noah, and the rope fell neatly round two tigers and two bears! How they roared and growled! They bit through the rope in a twinkling, left the line of animals, and tore over to where Amelia was standing with the cowboy doll.

The bears bit the cowboy doll's shaggy trousers so hard that they

made a hole in them. The tigers scratched Amelia Jane on her legs, and you should have heard her yell!

'It serves you right,' said Tom, who had been watching. 'We've told you ever so many times not to keep lassoing people.'

So for a little while Amelia Jane was good, but then something happened that made her bad again.

Somebody left a bag of sweets on the nursery mantelpiece. They belonged to one of the children, and Nanny had put them there. Amelia Jane saw them and looked longingly at them, for she loved eating lots of sweets and chocolates.

How could she possibly get those sweets? She looked up at the mantelpiece and thought hard. The clock ticked away there. The goldfish globe winked back. It stood on the mantelpiece too, and was full of little black tadpoles that the children had found in the ponds. The china cat stood there too, watching the tadpoles wriggling about. And just by the cat was that bag of sweets.

'Oh, I know how I can get them!' said Amelia suddenly. 'I can lasso them with the cowboy's rope! Cowboy doll, where are you? Will you lend me your rope for a moment?'

The cowboy doll untied it. He always kept it tied round his waist. He gave it to Amelia Jane and asked her what she wanted it for.

'I'm going to lasso that bag of sweets on the mantelpiece and get it down here!' said naughty Amelia. 'Then we'll share the sweets, Cowboy doll!'

'You'd better let *me* do the lassoing,' said the cowboy. 'You'll only go and lasso the cat or the clock, Amelia Jane!'

'No, *I* want to do it,' said Amelia. She looked up at the mantelpiece and swung the rope carefully. Whizz! It flew up to the mantelpiece! It missed the bag of sweets. It missed the clock. It just missed the china cat, but it caught the goldfish bowl! It fell neatly round it. The rope was tight – it pulled at the bowl – it toppled it over!

The watching toys gave a shriek! The water poured out of the bowl – all over Amelia and the cowboy doll, who were just underneath! Tadpoles fell down their necks and flopped on to the floor! The bowl fell off too, and all the toys thought it would smash on the floor.

But no! It was too clever for that! It fell on to Amelia Jane's head, and there she stood, wet through, with the glass bowl on her head like an extra big hat!

Well, really, the toys simply couldn't *help* laughing! She looked too funny, and the cowboy doll, too, was soaked from head to foot. He was trying to get a tadpole which had fallen down his back and was tickling him dreadfully.

'Don't stand there laughing like this,' said Tom suddenly. 'Those tadpoles will die out of water. Quick, get something to put them into.'

The toys looked round for something but all they could think of was Amelia Jane's teacup. She was a big doll, so she had a very big cup. The toys put some water in it and then picked up the poor wriggling tadpoles. They found the one down the cowboy's neck, and took two from Amelia's neck as well. Dear, dear, what an excitement there was!

'What do you want to bother with

silly tadpoles for, when Amelia Jane and I are all wet through!' cried the cowboy doll crossly. 'Please dry us.'

'It is more important to save the tadpoles than to bother about *you*,' said the clown. 'You can dry yourselves. It was your own fault that all this happened. Amelia Jane had no right to try and lasso sweets that didn't belong to her!'

Amelia squeezed out of her wet things and took the bowl off her head. It was rather a tight fit, and at first she thought she might have to wear the bowl all her life! That did give her a shock. She stood by the fire and tried to dry herself. She felt very cold and sad. The cowboy doll was wet too, and very angry.

'You *are* silly,' he said to Amelia Jane. 'Why didn't you let me do the lassoing? I could have got the bag of sweets then, but all we got was cold water and tadpoles!'

Amelia Jane said nothing, but dear me, when she found that her teacup was full of swimming tadpoles she was horrified.

'How can I ever drink out of my nice cup again?' she wept. 'It will be all tadpoley.'

'Amelia Jane, stop being silly,' said Tom sternly. 'You have made enough mischief without being stupid too. What do you suppose Nanny will say when she finds the tadpoles upset and the bowl on the rug?'

Nanny said a lot. She simply could *not* understand what had happened! At first she thought it was the cat who had done it. But no, Tibs had been in the kitchen all the time. And then she caught sight of the cowboy doll who was standing in a corner, still very wet.

'I believe it's you, with your lasso, you naughty doll!' she said. 'Back you go to your own home!'

'Perhaps Amelia Jane will be good now that the cowboy doll has gone,' said the teddy to the clown. But I don't expect she will – do you?

Amelia Jane and the Plasticine

Now Amelia Jane had been good for a long time – so good that the golden-haired doll really wondered if Amelia was ill. But she wasn't ill; as the clown said, 'She was just boiling up for some more mischief!'

Amelia Jane had found the box of plasticine in the cupboard, and every night she played with the plasticine.

She sat in a corner by herself, and the other toys took no notice of her at all. Amelia Jane was clever with the plasticine – she could make flowers and shells and tables and chairs and all kinds of things, just as you can.

And then, of course, naughty ideas began to come into her mind. She had heard the teddy bear complaining that he had no tail. Suppose she made him one and stuck it on when he was asleep? He would think he had grown a tail, and what fun it would be to see him walking about proudly, showing off his beautiful new tail! What would he say when it came off?

Amelia Jane made a beautiful long tail of plasticine. It was brown to match the teddy bear's fur, and it had some pretty little blue spots here and there. Amelia Jane made some marks on it to make it look furry. It was finished at last. Amelia Jane grinned to herself and waited till she saw the teddy bear asleep in a corner.

Then she crept up to him with the plasticine tail. Nobody was about.

Amelia Jane quickly pressed one end
of the tail on to the teddy bear's back.
It stuck nicely. Then the naughty doll
ran back to her place in the cupboard.

Presently the clockwork clown
walked along to talk to the bear. He
saw the tail, and he stared as if he
couldn't believe his eyes!

'Hie, Teddy, Teddy, wake up!' he
shouted in excitement. 'You've grown
a fine tail! You have really!'

The teddy woke up with a jump.
When he saw his new tail, curling
round him like a cat's, he was so
surprised that he couldn't say a word
at first. Then he got up and bent
himself over to have a look at it.

'A tail at last!' he said. 'A real tail!

I always thought I might grow one, and now I have!'

'Tom, come and look at Teddy's beautiful new tail!' cried the clown. 'Do come! It's a fine one!'

Tom came, and the golden-haired doll – and Amelia went too.

'It's magnificent,' said Tom.

'It makes you look really handsome, Teddy,' said the golden-haired doll.

'How clever of you to grow it all by yourself!' said naughty Amelia Jane.

'Wasn't it clever of me!' said Teddy proudly, and he walked about showing his new tail to everyone. The clockwork mouse loved it, and the yellow duck said it was the longest she had ever seen. The bear was so happy that his boot-button eyes shone like lamps.

Not long afterwards the toys all sat down together to have cups of cocoa which the clockwork mouse had made for them on the stove in the dolls' house. Amelia Jane sat down beside the teddy – and whatever do you suppose she did? When the others were not looking she took hold of the bear's plasticine tail and with her clever fingers she made the end of it into a snake's head! Fancy that! It looked exactly like a snake now, with its mouth open and two little holes for eyes!

Tom saw it first and gave a shriek!
'Oooh! Look! Your tail has turned into
a snake, Teddy!'

The bear looked down in alarm –
and when he saw the snake's head on
the end of his tail he jumped up with a
yell.

'Oh! Go away, snake, go away!'

he shouted, and
he ran to the
other side of the
room. But, of
course, his tail
followed him, for
it was stuck on to him – and it looked
as if the snake was running after him
backwards! Poor Teddy! He was so
frightened. He didn't like snakes at
all, and to have his new tail turning
into one seemed very dreadful to him.

Well, Amelia Jane laughed till she
cried. It seemed funny to her to see
the teddy bear rushing about with a
snake-tail! The toys thought her very
unkind to laugh, and the golden-
haired doll shouted at her. But as

Amelia Jane could shout twice as hard, that wasn't much good!

'Take your tail off, silly, if you're afraid of it!' called Amelia Jane.

'How can you take off a thing that's growing on you, stupid!' yelled back the teddy.

Amelia Jane ran to the bear and jerked at his tail. It came off quite easily, of course, for it was only plasticine. She threw it out of the window. The toys looked on in surprise. Then they all cheered Amelia.

'How brave of you, Amelia Jane! How good of you to do that! Did it hurt, Teddy?'

'Not a bit,' said Teddy, in surprise.

'Oh, thank you, Amelia Jane. The snake might have bitten you. You are very brave.'

Amelia Jane didn't tell the toys that the tail had only been plasticine made by herself. No – the naughty doll said nothing at all, but let the toys make a fuss of her.

I'll think of another plasticine trick, she thought gleefully. And, as you can guess, it wasn't very long before she did!

She made a set of nice little chairs, all with seats and backs and four neat little legs. Then she went to the paintbox and got the red paint. She painted those little chairs a bright red, and really, they looked simply lovely when she had finished. But, of course, you couldn't sit down on them because they were only made of plasticine and would crumple up at once!

But they didn't look as if they were made of plasticine when they were bright red. They looked like wooden chairs. Amelia Jane set them all out neatly in the middle of the floor.

'What are those chairs for?' asked Tom, in surprise.

'I'm going to have a party,' said Amelia Jane, and she got a table from the dolls' house. Then she called to the toys, 'Do come and join my party. The cakes haven't come yet but they'll be here soon. Just come and sit down and wait a while, Toys!'

The toys were pleased, for they loved any sort of a party. They came running over to Amelia Jane. Even the clockwork mouse came, and so did the old blue rabbit who had only one eye and no whiskers at all.

'Do sit down,' said Amelia, waving her hand to the red chairs. 'I hope there are enough seats for you all!'

Everyone sat down – but oh, what a shock they got! Tom's chair sank down at once, all its legs broken! He landed with such a bump on the ground! The golden-haired

doll's chair tipped over backwards, and she bumped her head, and sat so hard on the plasticine that it stuck to her pretty blue frock. The clockwork mouse's chair crumpled up and he fell off and lost his key.

One by one all the red chairs gave way and tipped out the surprised toys. The clown didn't know what was happening and he clutched the back of his chair so hard that he squeezed up the plasticine it was made of and got it all over his arms! What a shock for him!

Amelia Jane thought it was so funny! She laughed and laughed and laughed.

'It isn't funny,' said Tom angrily.

'Is this a trick instead of a party?'

'Yes,' said Amelia Jane. 'Oh, Tom you did look funny tumbling on to the floor!'

'I suppose there are no cakes coming after all,' said the clown fiercely. 'And I suppose too that it was you who stuck on the teddy bear's tail, and made it of plasticine! You are a wicked doll and you deserve to be frightened yourself!'

'Oh, you can't frighten me!' said Amelia Jane. 'I'm not afraid of anything!'

But she was, you know – she was afraid of beetles! The toys knew this, and they made up their minds to punish her! They went to the

plasticine box, and the clown, who
was clever with his fingers, made lots
of big beetles, all with feelers on their
heads and six legs under their bodies!
The clown painted them black.

'This isn't a very kind thing to
do,' said the clown, as he finished
the last beetle, 'but really, Amelia
Jane is so naughty that we must
teach her a lesson. Where is she?'

'In the toy-cupboard, reading,'
said the mouse. The clown took up
the beetles and put them here and
there on the floor. Then he called
Amelia Jane.

'Amelia, Amelia, come quickly!'

Amelia Jane put down her book and rushed out of the cupboard – but when she saw those plasticine beetles she gave such a yell!

'Oooh! Ow! Beetles! Where have they come from? Take them away!'

The bear had tied a bit of black cotton to one beetle and he suddenly jerked this. The beetle jumped, and Amelia Jane screamed: 'It's coming after me! It's coming after me! Oooooooh!'

She rushed back into the toy cupboard and crouched in the darkest corner. And do you know, she didn't come out of the cupboard for two days, so the toys had a lovely time playing together without wondering what mischief Amelia Jane was up to!

They have taken away the beetles, of course, but Amelia Jane doesn't know that! She'll think twice before she gets into mischief again, won't she!

Stop it, Amelia Jane!

You might think that Amelia Jane would grow out of her bad ways, but she didn't. The day soon came when she felt bad again. It was the day that the pop-gun came to the nursery. The children had bought it and had been playing with it. It was great fun.

It was a wooden gun that had a cork fitted in at the end of it. When you pressed the trigger the cork flew out with a pop, but it didn't go far, because it was tied on to the gun with a piece of string. The children set up their wooden soldiers in a row and shot them down – bang! – with the pop-gun. The soldiers didn't mind, because it was what they were made for.

But when Amelia Jane got hold of the pop-gun that night and began shooting the cork at everyone, there was trouble!

'Stop it, Amelia Jane!' shouted the clockwork clown angrily, when his cap flew off into the coal-scuttle, shot there by the cork.

'Stop it, Amelia Jane!' cried Tom when he got the cork in his eye.

'Stop it, Amelia Jane!' squealed the engine. 'You're making my funnel loose with that cork – it keeps hitting it!'

But do you suppose Amelia Jane stopped? Of course not! She was enjoying herself far too much!

She shot at the castle of bricks and down they all fell! She shot at everything in the toy farmyard, and trees, animals, and farmer fell over flat. She shot at the clockwork mouse and gave him such a fright that he ran into the dolls' house and hid under a bed. Nobody could get him out.

The clockwork clown called the other toys to him. 'We've got to stop Amelia Jane!' he said. 'I'm tired of all this popping. That cork doesn't do much damage but it stings all the same.'

'What about shooting Amelia Jane?' asked Tom eagerly. 'I'd like to do that.'

'Oh, she won't let that pop-gun go, you may be sure of that!' said the teddy bear.

'Well, there's a funny old gun in the cupboard that the children got out of a cracker,' said the clockwork clown. 'Why not shoot at her with that?'

'Because it doesn't shoot, silly,'

said the bear. 'I've tried it heaps of times.'

'If it only made a pop it would do,' said the clown gloomily. 'We don't really want to shoot Amelia Jane – only to frighten her and make her stop popping the cork-gun at us.'

'Well, that old gun doesn't shoot and it doesn't make a pop either,' said Tom.

Then the bear had an idea. 'Listen!' he whispered, so that Amelia Jane wouldn't hear. 'I know where there is a packet of balloons! Couldn't we get them – and blow them up – and let Tom hide behind the curtain with them? Then I could hold the gun and point it at Amelia Jane – and at

the same moment Tom could prick a
balloon and burst it! Then it would go
– *bang*! just like a gun – and frighten
Amelia Jane!'

Everyone thought that was a
splendid idea. So Tom got the packet
of balloons and organised the toys to
blow them up. They hid behind the
curtains with the balloons. There were

five. The bear found the gun and polished it up. Amelia Jane saw him and laughed.

'*That* old gun won't shoot!' she said, and she aimed the pop-gun at Teddy and shot the cork so hard that one of his ears went crooked. He was very angry.

'Oh, so you think this old gun won't shoot!' he said. 'Well, you're wrong!'

He pointed the gun at Amelia Jane – and at the same moment Tom dug a pin into one of the blown-up balloons behind the curtain.

Bang! went the balloon – and Amelia Jane gave a shriek. She really thought the gun that Teddy was holding had gone off!

'I'm shot! I'm shot!' yelled Amelia Jane in a fright. Everyone laughed. Teddy pointed the gun at the naughty doll again. Bang! went another balloon behind the curtains. Amelia Jane squealed and ran away.

'I'm shot again! I'm shot again!' she yelled. Teddy laughed so

much that he nearly dropped the gun.

'Do you promise not to shoot anybody with that pop-gun again?' he said.

'No, I don't!' said Amelia Jane.

'All right then!' said Teddy, and he pointed the gun at her again. 'I'll go on shooting at *you* then.'

Bang! went a third balloon behind the curtain, and Amelia Jane screamed, 'I'm shot! I'm shot! He's shot me three times!'

Bang! went another balloon, and Bang! went the fifth balloon. Amelia Jane screamed so loudly that she quite deafened everyone. She fled into the toy-cupboard and wept bitterly.

'I won't shoot anyone any more.

Here's the old pop-gun!' she cried and she threw it out of the cupboard to the teddy bear. 'Stop shooting me! I'm wounded everywhere!'

When Amelia Jane next came out of the toy-cupboard the toys stared in astonishment – for the big doll had bandaged her arms and legs and head. She did look funny!

'You shot me five times and wounded me,' said Amelia Jane in a hurt voice. 'You ought to be very sorry.'

But the toys laughed and laughed and laughed. How could she be wounded when it was only balloons that went off pop and not the gun? Oh, Amelia Jane, you are just a humbug!

Amelia Jane Up the Chimney

Into the nursery where naughty Amelia Jane lived, came a little black kitten one day. Its eyes were green, its tail was fat and long, and its little paddy-paws were like velvet.

All the toys loved the kitten at once – but Amelia Jane loved it most of all! How she cuddled it! How she fussed it! How she stroked it from ears to tail-tip and tickled it under its soft black chin!

The kitten belonged to the housekeeper. It was a pretty, gentle little thing, and it let the toys do what they liked with it. The teddy found it a buttery crumb to nibble. The clockwork clown turned head over heels seven times running to make it laugh. Tom found the dolls' hairbrush and brushed its fur till it shone.

But Amelia Jane wanted the kitten all to herself. She pushed away the other toys, and as she was bigger than they were they fell down, flop! That was the worst of Amelia – she was always so rough!

'*I* want this kitten!' said Amelia Jane. 'Tiddles, Tiddles, purr to me, and to no one else!'

'You are very selfish, Amelia Jane,' said Tom. Amelia Jane stuck out her elbow and pushed him again. Down he went, flip-flop! You couldn't do anything with Amelia Jane when she was feeling like that.

'This kitten is mine when it comes into our nursery,' said Amelia. 'Nobody else is to play with it then.'

Well, the kitten quite enjoyed being made a fuss of by Amelia, but it did want to play with the other toys sometimes. Amelia just wouldn't let it. She caught it and put it on her knee to stroke as soon as ever it ran over to Tom or Teddy.

And one day Amelia Jane thought she would like to dress the kitten up in clothes out of the dolls' chest-of-drawers! Quite a lot of clean dolls' clothes were kept there. It was really rather exciting to pull open the drawers and see the dear little coats and dresses, the fussy little bonnets with ribbons on, the socks and the shoes of all colours!

Amelia Jane pulled out the whole lot. She would, of course!

'Just look at that!' groaned Tom. 'Untidy creature! She'll never put those clothes back again neatly. *We* shall have to do that!'

Amelia Jane soon had all the clothes on the floor. She wondered which would fit the little black kitten. What fun to dress her up, she thought!

'This dress will fit you nicely, Tiddles,' she said, picking up a little red frock. 'Oh, you will look sweet in it. And this yellow coat will fit you, too – and this little bonnet with ribbons! Oh, what a darling kitten you will look!'

'Mee-ow,' said Tiddles, not at all liking the idea of being dressed up by Amelia Jane. 'Mee-ow! I'm off!'

She shot to the nursery door – but Amelia Jane was too quick. She reached out her hand and caught poor Tiddles. 'You come here!' she said. 'I'm going to make you look really sweet!'

Well, Tiddles had to sit and be dressed up. First Amelia put on the little red frock and did all the buttons up the back. Then she put on the yellow coat. She tied a ribbon round Tiddles' waist. Then she put the bonnet on Tiddles' little black head and tied it on firmly.

'There!' she said. 'You are now a little dolly cat! You look lovely! Look, everybody!'

Everybody came to look. They couldn't help thinking that Tiddles really did look rather sweet – but

Tiddles hated it! She struggled and wriggled and tried her hardest to scrape off her bonnet. She didn't like anything over her ears. She couldn't hear properly.

'Now, you shall look at yourself in the mirror, Tiddles,' said Amelia Jane, and she carried the dressed-up kitten to the big mirror.

The kitten looked at herself – and when she saw herself looking so very strange, with a bonnet on her ears, and a coat and dress hiding her black fur, she was afraid.

'Mee-ow! It isn't me!' she said in a fright, and she rushed away to go downstairs to the housekeeper. But Amelia Jane pushed the door shut.

'You're not to go away, Tiddles,' she said. 'We want to see you walking about nicely in your new clothes.'

But that was just what Tiddles couldn't and wouldn't do! She caught sight of herself in the mirror again and ran off in terror. She was so frightened that she meant to get out of the nursery somehow! But how could she? The door was shut. The window was shut.

'Oh, where can I go-ee-ow?' mewed poor Tiddles.

Now it was summer-time, so there was no fire in the nursery grate. Tiddles leapt over the guard, and in a moment she scrabbled up the chimney and was gone!

The toys stared at one another in alarm. What would happen to Tiddles up the chimney?

'Are you all right, Tiddles?' called Tom, sticking his head up the chimney.

'No-ee-oh-ee-ow!' wailed poor Tiddles, who was more frightened than ever up the dark chimney. She didn't dare to go up and she didn't dare to go down! Poor Tiddles!

The toys turned fiercely on naughty Amelia Jane. 'It's your fault!' shouted Teddy. 'You would dress her up and frighten her, just to amuse yourself. Now what are we to do?'

'Oh-ee-ow-ee-oh!' wailed Tiddles, up the chimney.

'I know! We'll make Amelia Jane go up the chimney and fetch Tiddles!' cried Tom. 'That's what we'll do!'

'I won't go,' said Amelia Jane.

'Oh yes, you will!' said Teddy. 'Come on, everyone. Push Amelia up the chimney!'

But they couldn't get the big doll to go. She just wouldn't be pushed. Just as the toys were going to have another push at Amelia, someone opened the nursery door. It was the housekeeper!

The toys at once lay down flat on the floor and kept quite still.

'I wonder where that kitten of mine is,' said the housekeeper, looking round the nursery. 'I thought I heard her mewing up here.'

'Oh-ee-ow-ee-ow!' wailed Tiddles from the chimney. The housekeeper looked astonished. 'I believe she's up the chimney!' she said. Then someone called her from downstairs and she hurried away.

Now Amelia Jane, although she really was a very naughty doll, was feeling most uncomfortable about poor Tiddles, for she was fond of her.

As soon as the housekeeper had gone she ran across to the fireplace, climbed over the guard, and looked up the chimney.

'I'm going up the chimney to rescue Tiddles,' she said to the surprised toys. 'I'm not going because you tried to push me up – I'm going because I don't like Tiddles to be frightened.'

And up the chimney went Amelia Jane! The toys listened to her scrabbling her way up the long, dark,

119

sooty chimney. Bits of soot fell down and one bit hit the teddy on the nose. 'The chimney wants sweeping,' he said.

'Looks as if Amelia is sweeping it!' said Tom, as another bit of soot rolled down.

At last Amelia Jane reached Tiddles who sat in a sooty corner, trembling. Amelia Jane put her arm round the kitten and hugged her. 'I'll help you to get down,' she said.

But dear me, that wasn't easy! Amelia Jane lost her way in the chimney, which joined all sorts of other chimneys here and there! Tiddles clung to her with all her claws and Amelia felt as if she was being pricked with twenty needles!

Now, very soon, the housekeeper came into the nursery again, and who do you suppose was with her? The sweep! Yes – the housekeeper had told him a kitten was up the chimney, and he had said he would try to sweep her out very gently.

He screwed on the handles of his big brush one after another, and the brush went higher and higher up the chimney. Amelia Jane heard it coming. She didn't know the chimney was being swept. The toys had all rushed into the cupboard when they heard the housekeeper and the sweep coming upstairs! They hadn't had time to tell her anything.

'Oooh! What's this coming up the chimney?' suddenly said Amelia, as she dimly saw something black and hairy coming nearer and nearer. She didn't know it was the sweep's round black brush! 'Oooh! It's got whiskers! It's touched me! It's pushing me!'

Poor Amelia Jane! She was just as frightened as the kitten had been when it first ran up the chimney! She couldn't get away from the brush. It lifted her and the kitten up, up, and up!

'It's caught me, it's caught me!' wept Amelia. 'I didn't know a whiskery thing lived in chimneys!'

The brush swept Amelia Jane and the kitten right out of the chimney into the air! The kitten fell to the roof on its feet, and made its way carefully down to the kitchen, where the housekeeper took off the dolls' clothes in much astonishment.

Amelia didn't fall on her *feet*, because she wasn't a cat but a doll! She slid down the roof. She hung for a moment in the gutter. She fell over the gutter – down, down, down – and into the prickly holly bush that grew just below!

'Ooh-ee-ow-ee-oh!' yelled Amelia, for the holly bush pricked her well! She scrambled out somehow and after a long time got back to the nursery.

But when she crept in at the door, what a fright she gave the toys! She was covered in soot from head to toe. Her clothes were all torn! Her face and arms were pricked and scratched!

'Oooooh!' yelled the toys and rushed to shut themselves in the cupboard. 'What is it? What is it?'

'It's me, Amelia Jane,' said Amelia, in a very small voice. 'I've come back.'

'Well, you look DREADFUL!' said Teddy, sticking his head out of the cupboard. 'For goodness' sake undress and have a bath and put on clean clothes!'

So Amelia did – but the clothes in the dolls' chest were much too small for her, and she did look funny walking about in things belonging to the baby doll!

'I shall be good in future,' said Amelia Jane. But I don't believe it, do you?

Amelia Jane and the soap

Amelia Jane was feeling very bored. She had behaved herself for a whole week!

'But only because she hasn't been able to think of anything naughty to do,' said Tom to Teddy. 'As soon as she thinks of something she'll cheer up and be as bad as ever.'

Well, it wasn't long before Amelia

Jane did cheer up. She had thought of something.

You see, it was like this – she had gone out for a nice walk, sitting in the dolls' pram, and she had been taken into the town. Now, racing up and down the pavement were two boys on roller-skates. What a pace they went!

Amelia Jane leaned out of the pram to watch them. She thought it was a lovely game. She tried to see what the boys had on their feet, but they went so fast that Amelia Jane really didn't see what the skates were like.

How *do* they slip along so fast? she thought. I *would* like to skate like that. How I wish I could! I'd go round and round the nursery, and down the passage and back. My, wouldn't the toys stare!

Now, when Amelia Jane had an idea she just had to carry it out. So when she got back to the nursery she sat at the back of the toy-cupboard and thought hard.

'I want to skate,' she said to herself. 'I want to put something on my feet and slip along like those boys. I want to go fast! But what can I put on my feet?'

'What are you thinking so hard about?' asked the clockwork clown, poking his head in at the door.

'Never you mind,' said Amelia Jane.

'Tell me, and maybe I can help,' said the clown.

'Well, I'm trying to think of something nice and slippery,' said Amelia Jane.

'What about jelly?' said the clown.

'Don't be silly,' said Amelia.

'Well, soap,' said the clown. 'Nice wet soap! Why, the other day I got hold of some wet soap and squeezed it – and it shot out of my hand like lightning and hit Tom on the ear!'

Amelia Jane laughed. Then she

stopped and thought quickly. Soap!
Yes – that was really a *good* idea! If
she got two nice pieces of soap, made
them wet and slippery and tied them
under her feet, she would be able to
slip along just like those boys on
skates! Good!

'I'll try it!' said Amelia Jane. So
she ran out of the toy-cupboard and
went to the nursery basin. She
climbed up and looked to see if there

was any soap there. There was – and
what luck! – it had broken into two
nice pieces.

'Oooh!' said Amelia, in delight.
'Just what I want!'

She turned on the tap and wetted
the soap till it was so slippery she
could hardly hold it. Then she
climbed down with it. The toys looked
at her in amazement.

'What are you going to do?' said

Teddy. 'Are you going to give yourself a good wash for once?'

'Don't be rude,' said Amelia. 'You'll see in a minute what I'm going to do.'

She took off a hair-ribbon and tore it in two. Naughty Amelia! Then she tied one piece of soap under her right foot and the other piece under her left foot. The toys stared at her as if they thought she was mad.

'Amelia, that's a funny way of washing your feet,' said Tom at last.

'I'm not washing my feet. I'm

going to *skate*!' said Amelia proudly. 'Turn back the carpet, somebody. I must skate on the polished floor.'

The toys began to giggle. Really, what *would* Amelia Jane do next! Teddy and Tom turned back the carpet. Unfortunately they rolled the clockwork mouse up in it and had to unroll it again to get him out.

'Oh, do be quick!' said Amelia impatiently. 'I am simply longing to begin!'

At last the carpet was rolled right back. Amelia Jane began. She put first one foot out – slid along a little way on the soap – then put the other foot forward and slid too – and before the toys knew what she was about, there she was, skating round the nursery on her soap-skates!

How the toys laughed! Really, it was too funny to see Amelia sliding along so fast on pieces of soap!

Amelia Jane tried to stop – but she toppled and fell over, bang! The toys roared. It was funny to watch Amelia sitting down, plop, glaring at them angrily.

'How dare you laugh at me!' cried Amelia Jane. 'I shall go and learn how to skate in the passage. There is a nice polished floor there – I shall slide beautifully!'

'No, stay here,' said the clown, in alarm. 'You know quite well that somebody may go along that passage and see you, Amelia Jane.'

'Pooh, everyone's in bed,' said
Amelia, and this was true, for it was
past midnight. 'Anyway, you won't be
able to laugh at me there, if I fall
down – for none of you dares to come
into the passage.'

It was dark in the passage, for
only a small light burnt there. Amelia
slid out on her soap-skates and began
to slide gaily up and down, up and
down! The kitchen cat, hearing the
noise, came creeping up the stairs,
wondering if there was an extra-large-
size mouse anywhere about.

He *was* astonished when he saw
Amelia. He ran along the passage to
see what she had on her feet. Amelia

didn't hear him or see him, and she
suddenly bumped right into him.
Crash! She fell over and banged her

head against the bedroom door.

'Sh! Amelia Jane! Sh!' whispered
Tom, putting his head out of the
nursery door. But Amelia Jane

wouldn't hush. She got up angrily and shooed the cat away. But the cat spat and hissed, which scared her a bit.

If Amelia Jane had been sensible she would have run back to the nursery at once, but she was so keen on skating that she once more began to slide up and down, up and down, all along the passage. She didn't hear Nanny's bed creaking. She didn't hear Nanny creeping to the door. She didn't even see Nanny poking her head round the door – no, she went slipping and sliding up and down on the soap, having a perfectly lovely time!

Nanny couldn't make out who or what it was, for the passage was so dark. But she could quite well see something going up and down the passage, skating quickly. She moved to the light switch to put a brighter light on.

Amelia Jane saw her then. Quick as lightning the doll slipped through the nursery door, fell over on the carpet, tore off the bits of soap, and ran to the toy-cupboard. She climbed in on top of the bear and the clown, who were very angry at being walked on.

But nobody dared to say a word! Suppose Nanny had seen what was happening? But when Nanny turned on the big light, all she saw was the kitchen cat sitting calmly by the wall.

'Good gracious,' she said, 'so it was *you* I saw, Puss, skating up and down the passage! What do you mean by doing that in the middle of the night, I should like to know! My goodness, what is the world coming to, when cats take to sliding up and down passages and waking everybody up! Shoo! Shoo!'

She shooed the cat down the stairs, and he disappeared quickly, tail in air, boiling with rage to think that Amelia Jane had slipped off and left him to take the blame.

And in the morning, when Nanny saw the messy bits of soap lying on the carpet, she was crosser than ever.

'Just look at that!' she said to Jane,

the cleaner. 'It must be that cat. Slipped and slid down the passage all night long like a mad thing – and then went and tried to eat the soap out of the basin!'

Poor Puss got a scolding! Amelia Jane laughed at him – but she didn't laugh quite so much when the cat came downstairs and tore her new dress with his sharp claws.

'You'd better not skate any more with the soap, Amelia Jane,' said Tom. 'It's funny to watch you – but if you get other people into trouble it's not fair!'

So that was the end of Amelia Jane skating on the soap. I would have loved to see her, wouldn't you?

Amelia Jane and the Snow

It was snowing hard. The toys looked out of the nursery window and watched the big white snowflakes come floating down.

'The garden has a new white carpet,' said the teddy bear.

'Let's send the clockwork clown out to sweep the dust off it!' said Amelia Jane, the big naughty doll, with a giggle.

'Don't be silly, Amelia,' said the clown. 'You do say stupid things. There's no dust on a snow-carpet!'

'Isn't it pretty!' said the pink rabbit. 'I'd like to go and burrow in it!'

'Let's go and play in it!' said the golden-haired doll. 'It would be such fun.'

'Come on, then!' said Amelia

Jane. She ran to the door, peeped out, and beckoned the others. 'Nobody's about. We'll slip out of the garden door and go to the bit of garden behind the hedge. Nobody will see us there.'

'Stop a bit, Amelia Jane,' said the clockwork clown. 'Put on a coat. It's very cold outside.'

'Pooh!' said Amelia impatiently. 'Don't be such a baby, Clockwork Clown! I shall be as warm as toast running about. I'm going!'

She ran off down the stairs. But the other toys stayed to put on hats, coats, and scarves. Even the clockwork mouse put a red handkerchief round his neck.

When they got out to the snow they found that Amelia Jane had already made herself a great many snowballs! She danced about as they came, and shouted in glee.

'Let's have a snow-fight! Come on! I've got my snowballs ready. Look out, clown! Look out, pink rabbit!'

The big doll threw a snowball hard. It hit the clown on the head and he fell over, plonk! Amelia Jane giggled. She threw a snowball at the golden-haired doll and hit her in her middle. The doll gave a squeal and sat down in the snow.

'Ooh, this is fun!'

yelled Amelia. 'Come on, everyone, get some snowballs ready!'

But nobody could make such big hard snowballs as Amelia Jane. Amelia did enjoy herself. She pelted all the toys with snowballs, hitting them on the head and the chest and the legs – anywhere she could. She was quite a good shot, and the toys got very angry.

'Amelia Jane! Stop!' shouted Tom. 'It isn't fair. Your snowballs are three times as big as ours, and you make

them so hard that they hurt. Stop, I tell you!'

But Amelia

Jane wouldn't stop. No, she went on and on – and how she laughed when all the toys turned and ran away from her shower of snowballs!

'Let's leave her alone,' said the clown crossly. 'She's too tiresome for anything.'

'But she'll follow us and go on snowballing us,' said the mouse.

'No, she won't. She's found something else to snowball,' said the teddy bear. 'Look! She's snowballing the kitten!'

So she was. The kitten didn't mind the snowballs at all because she could always dodge them. She pounced on them as they fell, and Amelia Jane laughed to see her. She forgot about the toys.

'What shall we do?' said the golden-haired doll.

'Let's build a nice, round snow-house,' said the clown eagerly. 'It would be such fun to do that. I know how to. You just pile nice hard snow round in a ring and gradually make a round wall higher and higher. Then you make the wall slope inwards till the sides meet, and that's the roof!'

'Oh yes, that would be lovely!' said Tom. 'We could all live in the snow-house then.'

'But we won't let Amelia Jane come in at all,' said the clockwork mouse, getting a little snowball for the wall of the house.

'No, we won't,' said the golden-haired doll. 'It will punish her for throwing such hard snowballs at us.'

The toys worked hard at their snow-house. Soon the wall was quite high. It was a perfectly round wall. It grew higher and higher – and at last, as the toys shaped it to go inwards, the round sides met together and made a rounded roof.

The toys made a dear little doorway at the bottom. They were very excited, for the house was lovely. The clown ran to the pond, cut a square piece of ice, and ran back with it.

'What's that for?' asked the pink
rabbit.

'A window, of course!' said the

clown. He made a square hole in the
side of the house and fitted in the
piece of ice. It made a lovely window!

'Now let's go inside and be cosy,' said the golden-haired doll. So they all crowded into the dear little snow-house and sat down. It was lovely.

But just as the clockwork clown was telling a nice story, Amelia Jane came up. The kitten had gone indoors, and Amelia Jane wanted someone else to play with. She had looked and looked for the toys, but as they were in the snow-house she hadn't seen them.

She suddenly saw the house and came running up to it. She peeped inside the window.

'Oh, what a nice little house!' she cried. 'Let me come in, too!'

'No, Amelia Jane!' shouted all the

toys. 'You are too big. Besides, we don't want you.'

'But I'm very, very cold,' said Amelia Jane, and certainly she was shivering.

'Well, you should have been sensible and put on your coat and hat as we did!' said the golden-haired doll.

'Oh, *do* let me come in!' begged Amelia, who hated to be left out of anything. 'Oh, do let me!'

'NO, NO, NO!' shouted the toys.

'Well, I'm *coming* in!' said Amelia crossly, and she began to push her way in at the door. A bit of the doorway fell down at once.

'Don't!' cried the clown, in alarm. 'You will break our house!'

'Serve you right!' said naughty Amelia. But the toys really couldn't bear to see their house broken.

'All right, all right, you can come in,' said Tom. 'But wait till we get out, Amelia. You are so big that there isn't room for anyone else when *you're* inside!'

That pleased Amelia very much. She thought it would be lovely to have the house all to herself. She waited until all the toys had squeezed out of the house, and then she went in.

'Oh, it's lovely!' she cried. She pressed her nose to the window and looked out. 'It's lovely! It's a real little house. This shall be mine. You build another one for yourselves, Toys.'

But the toys were tired. They
stared angrily at Amelia Jane.

'You are a very naughty, selfish
doll,' shouted the teddy bear. 'First
you snowball us till we have to run
away. Then you take our house for
your own.'

'I'm cold,' said the clown,
shivering. 'Let's go and slide on the
ice for a bit. Perhaps Amelia will get

tired of our house soon and we can have it again.'

So they went off to the pond and left Amelia Jane by herself.

Amelia felt cold. She shivered and shook in the little snow-house. 'I wish there was a fire in this house,' she said to herself, 'then it would be nice and warm. I'll make one! How the toys will stare when they see I have a nice fire to warm myself by! But I shan't let them come in at all!'

She ran to the wood-shed and got some wood. She found some matches there that the gardener used when he lit a bonfire. She ran back to the snow-house. Soon the twigs were crackling loudly.

'What's that noise?' said the clown suddenly. All the toys stopped their sliding and listened. It came from their snow-house.

'Amelia Jane is lighting a fire there!' said Tom. Then the toys looked at one another – and began to giggle. They knew quite well what would happen if anyone lit a fire in a house made of snow! They ran up to watch.

'You can't come in, you can't come in!' shouted Amelia Jane. 'This is my house, and this is my own dear little warm fire! Oh, I'm so cosy! Oh, I'm so warm!'

The toys stood and watched. The fire blazed up as the twigs burnt.

There was a red glow inside the little house. It certainly looked very cosy. Amelia Jane put out her hands and warmed them inside the house.

But something was happening. The fire was melting the house! After all, it was only made of snow! The walls began to drip. The roof began to drip. The bit of ice that was the window disappeared altogether.

Amelia Jane felt the drips on her back and was cross.

'Who's pouring water on me?' she cried. 'Stop it, or I'll be very angry!'

Drip, drip, drip went the snow as it melted all around her. And suddenly the whole house fell in, for the snow was now so soft and melty that it

couldn't hold together. The fire went
out with a sizzle.

Amelia Jane disappeared, for the
snow fell all over her!

'Oooh! Ow! What's happened?'
yelled Amelia Jane, very frightened.

She kicked about in the wet snow, and first her hands came out, and then her head. She sat in the snow and looked around.

'Ha ha! Ho ho ho!' roared the toys. 'It serves you right, Amelia Jane! You took our house – and you lit a fire and melted it – and it fell on top of you! Ha ha! Ho ho ho!'

Amelia Jane began to cry. She was wet through and very cold. She ran back to the nursery, leaving little wet marks all the way. She sat by the fire there and tried to get dry.

And very soon she began to sneeze: 'A-tishooo! A-tishoo!'

'Now I've got a cold!' she said miserably. 'Oh, why do I get naughty? Something nasty always happens to me when I do!'

'Well, just try and remember that, next time you feel naughty,' said Tom, giving Amelia his big red handkerchief.

But I don't expect she'll remember it, do you?

Amelia Jane Goes Mad

Once, when Amelia Jane, that big rascal of a doll, had been good for simply ages, she suddenly got tired of it and went quite mad! Never in her life had she been so naughty and, really, the toys got quite scared of her!

She was quite silly over water. She thought it was the greatest fun to fill the watering-can that belonged to the children, and lie in wait for any toy to come by at night.

She hid behind the curtain and waited till Tom came by. Then she tilted up the little green can and watered him! Goodness, how he jumped!

'It's raining!' he cried, and ran to get his umbrella. But when he put it up, no rain fell at all, and everyone laughed at him.

'It never rains in the nursery, silly!' said the clockwork clown.

'Well, look at my wet hair,' said

Tom, and he shook a shower of drops all over the clown. 'What do you call that if it isn't rain?'

The clockwork clown snorted, and went to visit the clockwork mouse over in the corner. He didn't know that Amelia Jane was hiding behind the scuttle with the watering-can again! Just as he came by, whistling a merry little tune, Amelia tilted up the can – and, pitter-patter! down came the water over the startled clown.

He ran to get the umbrella then – and holding it carefully over him, he went back to the scuttle to find out what the water was. And there, of course, he found Amelia, laughing till the tears ran down her cheeks.

'Give me that watering-can, Amelia Jane,' said the clockwork clown sternly. When he spoke like that, he had to be obeyed, so Amelia meekly gave him the can. But she soon began to look around for some more water to play with.

This time she found a very naughty thing to do. She found that if she stood on a chair by the wash-basin and turned on the tap, she could make the water spurt out all over the room by putting her hand under the tap. And she waited till the golden-haired doll came by, and then spurted the water all over her!

The golden-haired doll was angry, because the water went on her hair and took out the curl. So she was a straight-haired doll then, and everyone thought she looked most peculiar.

'I shall have to put my hair in curl-papers tonight, and they are so uncomfortable,' sighed the doll. 'Oh, how I wish I could *punish* Amelia Jane!'

Well, the clown climbed up to the basin, and with his strong hands he turned off the two taps so very tightly that not even Amelia Jane could turn them on again. So she couldn't play *that* trick any more.

Never mind! thought Amelia. I shall think of something else! What fun it is to play with water!

Well, she just couldn't get any water from the taps, and the toys felt safe. But Amelia Jane knew somewhere else to get water. Yes – the goldfish bowl was full of water for the two goldfish to swim in!

The goldfish lived on a table by the wall. Amelia Jane climbed up to the wash-basin and took the sponge from there. It was quite dry. Then she climbed up to the goldfish bowl and looked into the water.

'Can I borrow some of your water?' she asked the fish. And then, without waiting for an answer, she dipped the sponge into the water and made it dripping wet.

Amelia sat on the table and

peeped over
the edge,
waiting
for
someone to
come by.
The rabbit
and the dog
were having a
little walk together
and were coming
near. Amelia Jane
giggled.

She waited until they
were just underneath,
and then she squeezed
the sponge gently.
Drip-drip-drip, drop-

drop-drop! Large cold drops of water fell on to the dog and the rabbit. They were most surprised. They looked up – but Amelia was no longer peeping over the edge of the table, and they could see nothing. They couldn't understand it.

'I'm wet,' said the rabbit, shaking himself.

'And I'm wet too,' said the dog, licking himself. 'Where did it come from?'

'Can't imagine,' said the rabbit. 'Perhaps we are mistaken. Come, let us go on with our ramble.'

So on they went again, and Amelia Jane watched for them to come back near the table once more.

Just as they passed, she held out her sponge and squeezed it hard again.

Drip-drip-drip, drop-drop-drop! Down came the water and soaked the dog and the rabbit. How angry they were!

'My ears are dripping,' said the rabbit.

'My whiskers are soaked,' said the dog. 'Let us tell the clown.'

Well, as soon as they complained to the clown, he knew quite well it must be Amelia Jane up to her water-tricks again, and he called to her very sternly:

'Amelia Jane! Will you stop soaking everyone? It isn't funny, it is very silly, for you will give everyone a dreadful cold. Where are you?'

But Amelia Jane wouldn't answer, though she was aching with trying to stop laughing. The clown was angry, and set out to look for her. He came too near the table and Amelia Jane saw him.

'I can't help it!' she said to herself. 'I must throw this nice wet sponge at him!'

So she threw the sponge at the clown, and it hit him full in the middle. He fell down with a thud, and the sponge dripped wet on him from top to toe. He got up and stared angrily round. But he could *not* see Amelia Jane. She was crouching down on the top of the table again, behind the goldfish bowl.

The clown went to talk to the doll, whose hair was now in curl-papers. The rabbit, the dog, Tom, and the clockwork mouse came too.

'It's time we stopped Amelia Jane,' said the clown. 'What about doing something to *her* with water? That would really be a good punishment!'

'But how can we?' asked the doll with curl-papers. 'If we throw the sponge at her, she'll only throw it back. And you've hidden the can so that she can't get it.'

Everybody thought hard. And then the clockwork mouse had an idea! He was only a small toy, but he sometimes had surprisingly big ideas.

'I know!' he said. 'What about a siphon of soda-water?'

All the toys stared at him as if he were quite mad. '*You* know!' said the mouse. 'The thing that the big people keep in the dining-room, and squirt into a glass when they want a drink. I've seen them. What about getting one of those out of the kitchen where they are stored, and having a squirt at Amelia Jane? If she's so fond of water, she might like a bit of squirting!'

The toys laughed. The clockwork clown and the rabbit went out of the nursery and down the passage to the kitchen to see if they could find a siphon. They found one quite easily in the larder. It was terribly heavy. They had to fetch the dog to help them to carry it back to the nursery.

Amelia Jane had got down from the table and was busy tying a new hair-ribbon in her yellow hair. She was surprised to hear the heavy bumping as the toys carried the siphon in at the door. She turned round and laughed.

'Whatever have you brought that great ugly thing for?' she asked.

'Do you want to know?' said the clown, bringing it right up to her. Before she could answer, the toys pressed on the handle of the siphon, and the soda-water squirted out with a tremendous hissing noise, right into

Amelia Jane's surprised face!

Good gracious! She was so startled
that she fell over! The toys squealed
with delight and squirted her on the
ground. She got up and ran away in
a dreadful fright. But the toys
followed her, and squirted her all the
way! Oh dear, oh dear! Poor Amelia,
what a shock she got! The siphon
made such a noise, and the water
soaked her and ran down her neck
and quite took her breath
away!

'Do you like water so much now?' cried the clown. 'Do you think it is nice to be soaked? Squirt-squirt-squirt! How do you like to be watered, Amelia Jane?'

Well, Amelia certainly did *not* like it! She squealed and screamed and made such a noise that the toys were really afraid she would wake up everyone who was asleep. So they stopped squirting her and quietly took the siphon back to the kitchen.

Poor Amelia Jane! She had to take off all her clothes, even her underwear, and dry them by the fire. Even her body was wet, and she had to dry that too, turning herself round and round all night long! I don't think she will play with water again, somehow!

And nobody in the house could think where all the soda-water out of that siphon had gone to. Amelia Jane isn't likely to tell them, anyhow!

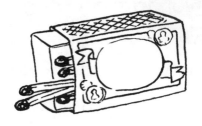

Amelia Jane and the Matches

This is the tale of Amelia Jane and the matches.

Now all boys and girls, unless they are quite old, are warned by their fathers and mothers never to play with matches. And with toys it is just the same. They must never play with matches, in case they get on fire and burn themselves.

But you can guess that Amelia
Jane didn't care about any danger!
No! If she could get hold of matches
you may be sure she would!

There were never any matches left
in the nursery, till one day when Jane
lit the fire and forgot to put the
matches back in her apron pocket, as
she usually did.

Jane left the box of matches on the
mantelpiece and Amelia Jane saw it
first, of course because she was quite
the tallest toy in the nursery.

'Oooh!' she said, pointing
upwards. 'Matches! If only I could get
them!'

'Don't be naughty,' said the
clockwork clown at once. 'You know

that children and toys must never touch matches.'

'Pooh!' said Amelia Jane rudely.

'Don't pooh at me like that!' said the clockwork clown. 'It's rude.'

'Pooh, pooh, pooh!' said Amelia Jane. So you can guess she was in one of her naughty moods again.

She stood and thought for a minute. Then she remembered how the cowboy doll had taught her to throw a lasso round anything and jerk it near. If only she could make a loop of rope and throw it carefully, she could get those matches down easily.

She ran to the string-box and opened it. The teddy bear saw her. 'If you're thinking of lassoing those matches and getting them down, just let me remind you what happened last time you tried your hand at that!' he said. 'You lassoed the bowl of tadpoles, and got them all down your neck.'

Amelia Jane took no notice. She got out a long piece of string and made a loop-knot at the end. Then she stood beneath the mantelpiece and threw the string neatly upwards, holding one end in her hand.

'Ooooh!' said all the toys in surprise, because, will you believe it, Amelia Jane got the loop right round the box, and it fell almost at her feet when she pulled the string!

'Aren't I clever!' said Amelia proudly.

'No, you're not, you're just lucky,' said the clockwork clown. 'You're not to touch those matches, Amelia Jane.'

'Pooh!' said Amelia, and she opened the box. 'Now, who wants to see me strike a match?'

The toys felt frightened. They knew quite well that matches can set fire to things and burn them. They ran to the toy-cupboard and crept inside, all except the clockwork mouse, and he did badly want to see a match struck.

'I'd like to see some matches struck, please, Amelia,' he said, and he ran nearer.

'Well, you shall see a whole lot struck!' said the big doll. 'The others have all run away, the sillies. You and I will enjoy ourselves!'

Amelia opened the box. She took out a match. She struck it hard on the side of the box. Fizzz-zzz-zzz! The match lit and Amelia Jane held it up in the air, watching the bright flame.

The clockwork mouse liked it very much indeed. He thought it was most exciting.

'Please, please, let me light one too,' he begged.

'Amelia Jane, if you let the mouse strike a match we'll all come out of the cupboard and punish you,' shouted the clockwork clown. 'He's too little to do dangerous things like that.'

'All right, all right!' said Amelia, striking another match. 'I shan't let him. Besides, I want to strike them all myself!'

But before Amelia Jane could strike any more matches there came the sound of steps on the landing outside. The toys flopped down. Amelia ran to the cupboard, throwing the box of matches into a corner. The clockwork mouse ran into the brick-box. So when

Jane looked into the nursery, there was no one to be seen at all. Everything was quiet. She had come to put some fresh flowers on the table. Then she dusted round a bit and went downstairs again.

The toys didn't come out for a long time – not until it was night, for they were afraid of being caught. The first toy that came alive was the clockwork mouse. He saw the box of matches in the corner and was pleased. He ran to them and pushed them along with his nose till he came to a slipper. He popped them into the slipper.

Aha! he thought. Now no one will know where they are, and I can strike as many as I like when the others are not looking!

Now when all the toys came out of the cupboard they looked very stern indeed. They were angry with Amelia Jane. She had no right to teach the clockwork mouse to play with matches!

The toys sat round Amelia in a circle, and scolded her.

'We shall none of us talk to you for a week,' said the teddy bear.

'We shall not play with you at all,' said the clockwork clown.

'You will not have any of the sweets out of the toy sweet-shop,' said the golden-haired doll.

'And we have hidden your fine new bonnet so that you can't wear it when you go out,' said the pink rabbit.

'Pooh!' said Amelia Jane – but not in a very poohy voice. She was upset. She hated not being talked to or played with. It would be horrid not to have any sweets. And oh, fancy hiding her lovely new bonnet so that she couldn't wear it! Amelia Jane felt like crying. She walked over to the window-seat and sat there, sniffing hard. She was very unhappy.

Suddenly the toys heard a curious noise.

Fizz-zz-zz-zz!

It was the clockwork mouse

striking a match all by himself. The toys stared at him in horror. He struck another and squeaked in delight.

But oh, my goodness me, what do you think happened?' His whiskers caught alight! Yes, they really did, and the poor little mouse found himself on fire, with flames burning each side of his little face!

'Sizzle-sizzle!' went his fine whiskers. The mouse squealed in fright and flung away the lighted match. Oh dear – it fell on to an open book and the pages caught alight! The book flamed up, and set light to the brick-box nearby.

'Crackle-crackle!' went the flames merrily. 'Crackle-crackle! We're going to eat the book! We're going to eat the brick-box! Then we'll eat the carpet – and the chairs – and the toy-cupboard – and all the toys – and the whole house! Crackle, crackle, crackle!'

It was dreadful. The toys stared in horror and couldn't move even a paw, they were so frightened. No wonder they had been warned against playing with matches. This was what happened when they disobeyed!

'Eee-eee-eee!' squealed the poor little clockwork mouse, his whiskers burning all away. He ran to and fro in pain and fright. All the toys watched and trembled dreadfully.

And what about that big, naughty

doll, Amelia Jane? Yes – she was watching too, her face pale with fright. Poor, poor little mouse – how she wished she hadn't shown him how to strike matches! And oh, that book – and the lovely brick-box! Whatever would happen to them all?

'Well, I began it, so I must try and stop it!' cried Amelia Jane. 'I remember hearing someone say that if anyone got on fire they should be rolled round tightly in a rug to put the flames out. Where, oh, where is a rug?'

'In the dolls' pram!' yelled the teddy bear, who was still too frightened to move.

Amelia Jane ran to the dolls' pram.

She snatched up the thick blue rug
there and rushed to the little
clockwork mouse. She threw the rug
all round his little grey body and
rolled him up tightly in it, head, tail,
and all! She felt the flames trying to
burn her hands, and they hurt her,
but she didn't stop. She meant to save
the little mouse!

The thick rug squashed all the
flames out. They died away. There
were none left. The clockwork mouse
wasn't on fire any more.

But the book and the brick-box
were still burning away. Amelia Jane
left the mouse and ran to the basin
with a jug. She stood on a chair,
turned on the tap and filled the jug.
Down she climbed and rushed to the
brick-box. She threw the water over
the flames.

'Sizzle-sizzle!' they said, and died
out. They could not go on burning
when water was thrown over them.
Then Amelia fetched another jug of
water and threw it over the burning
book.

'Sizzle-sizzle!' said the flames again, and went out. The fire was gone!

The toys came round, looking quite pale. Amelia Jane sat down and began to cry.

'I wish I hadn't touched the matches, I wish I hadn't!' she sobbed.

'I've got no whiskers now!' wept the poor little clockwork mouse. Sure enough, he hadn't – and he did look funny without them. What a noise Amelia Jane and the mouse made, sobbing together!

'You'll never speak to me or play with me again,' wept Amelia, looking round at the toys. 'I might as well go away from here and never come back.'

'Now listen, Amelia Jane,' said the teddy bear, putting his arm round her. 'You did a very wrong thing, and it has caused a lot of damage – but you have done your best to put it right, and you were brave when all of us were too afraid to do anything.'

'So we will have to forgive you,' said the clown. 'We were angry with you when you were bad, but we think you are brave too, so cheer up.'

'What about the mouse's whiskers, though – and the burnt book and brick-box?' wept Amelia.

'The mouse will have to do without his whiskers,' said Tom. 'The book was very old and torn, so perhaps it won't matter being burnt; and as for the brick-box, it's only the lid that has been burnt, and I can make a new one with the carpenter's set in the toy cupboard. But look at your own hands – and the front of your dress! They are burnt too!'

'It serves me right,' said Amelia

Jane. 'I'll put some good ointment on my hands, and I'll have to go about with a burnt bit of dress in front. Oh, I'm so glad you've forgiven me, Toys! I won't be naughty again.'

Well, the toys didn't believe *that*, of course – they knew Amelia Jane too well! But they were soon good friends again, and, secretly, they couldn't help admiring Amelia Jane for putting out the fire so quickly, and saving the little mouse.

'She's like the little girl in the nursery rhyme,' said the bear to the clown. '*You* know – when she's good she's *very, very* good – but when she's bad she's horrid!'

BOOK TWO

Amelia Jane Again!

Contents

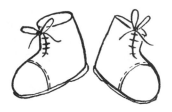

Amelia Jane and the shoes

Now once the toys in the nursery had a party and they didn't ask that big naughty doll, Amelia Jane. She didn't even know they were going to have a party until she saw them setting the table, and smelt the cakes cooking on the little stove in the dolls' house.

'Oooh!' said Amelia Jane, pleased. 'A party! This *is* a surprise!'

The teddy bear looked at her. 'It

will be an even greater surprise to you when you find you're not coming!' he said. 'We're a bit tired of you and your tricks. A party will be very nice without you!'

'Eeee-eee-eee!' laughed the clockwork mouse, and the other toys giggled too. Amelia Jane went red.

'You nasty, horrid things!' she said. 'Well, have your party then! I'm sure I don't want to come. I've better things to do than come to silly little parties like yours!'

She went off into the corner in a huff. The toys giggled again. Amelia Jane was funny when she was in a huff. She pouted her mouth and wrinkled her nose and tossed her thick yellow hair.

The party began. It was a lovely one, with tiny chocolate cakes to eat, small pink sweets out of the toy sweetshop, and lemonade to drink. The toys played blindman's-buff, and musical chairs, and general post, so they really did have a fine time. Amelia Jane pretended to be reading a book, but all the time she was really peeping at the party, and making up her naughty little mind that she would think of some trick to punish the little toys.

Now after a bit the toys wanted to dance. It was quieter to dance with their shoes off, so they all sat down, took off their shoes, and piled them in a heap near the dolls' house. Then they set the musical-box going, and began to dance with one another.

Amelia Jane saw the shoes in a big pile. She grinned to herself. What would the toys say if those suddenly disappeared? That would be funny!

So, when the toys were all busy dancing in and out and round about, Amelia Jane crept up to the shoes, stuffed them into the apron of her dress, and ran off again. Nobody noticed her.

Amelia Jane sat in a dark corner of the nursery with the shoes, wondering

where to hide them. Nearby was a
mouse-hole.

Oooh! thought Amelia. If I stuff
these shoes down the mouse-hole, no
one will find them. What fun!

So she stuffed the little shoes down
the mouse-hole. There were leather
shoes and woollen socks, kid shoes
and felt shoes, some with laces, some
with buttons, some with nothing at
all. They all went down that
mousehole.

Well, when

the dancing was over the toys ran to put their shoes on again. But they weren't there! They stared all around, very puzzled.

'I'm sure we put them here,' said the clockwork clown.

'Well, where are they?' asked the curly-haired doll. 'Shoes can't walk!'

'That's just what they can do!' said the clockwork mouse smartly.

'Not unless there are feet in them,' said the teddy bear, rather crossly. He wore woollen socks, and they kept his feet warm at night. He did hope they weren't lost.

'I'm sure Amelia Jane knows something about our shoes,' said the clockwork clown suddenly. The toys went over to her.

'Amelia Jane, what have you done with our shoes?' asked the teddy bear.

Amelia Jane looked so surprised that her eyebrows shot up into her hair. '*Shoes*!' she said. 'Shoes! Whatever do you mean?'

'Oh come, Amelia, you know quite well what shoes are!' said the clown crossly. 'What – have – you – done – with – our – SHOES?'

'Well, really!' said Amelia Jane. 'Why should you think I've done anything with them? Do you suppose I came and took them off your feet?'

'No, we don't suppose anything so silly,' said the bear. 'But we do feel perfectly sure you've taken the pile of shoes and hidden them somewhere.'

'Well, you can go on supposing,' said Amelia Jane rudely, and she began to read her book again. Not another word would she say.

The toys hated going without their shoes. Their feet were cold, and the teddy bear trod on a pin and yelled so loudly that the jack-in-the-box sprang out to see what the matter was. Not until the next night did Amelia Jane say what she had done.

All the toys were round her, begging for their shoes, and Amelia Jane looked at them, her cheeky face red with delight. 'Yes, I *did* take your shoes!' she said. 'I thought I would punish you for not asking me to your party.'

'Well, where did you *put* them?' asked the bear impatiently. 'Hurry up and tell us.'

'I pushed them down the mouse-hole,' said Amelia Jane, grinning.

'Pushed them down the *mouse*-hole!' cried all the toys, in astonishment. 'Oh, you naughty doll! Get them at once.'

'Get them yourself,' said Amelia Jane. '*I'm* not going to bother!'

So the clockwork mouse was sent into the mouse-hole to fetch out everybody's shoes. But, oh dear, oh dear, when he came back with them one by one, what an upset there was!

The little brown mice down the hole had bitten and chewed the shoes, meaning to make their new nest of them – and they were full of holes now.

'How dreadful!' groaned the clown. 'They're quite spoilt. Oh, you are a very naughty girl, Amelia Jane! Look at our shoes!'

Amelia was really sorry to see what had happened, but she wouldn't say so.

The toys put on their shoes, and went back to the toy-cupboard, very upset.

The next day, when the children saw the nibbled shoes, they were most surprised. 'Look!' they said. 'The mice have been eating our toys' shoes.

What a shame! We will take some money out of our money-box and buy them some more, and we'll knit the bear some nice new socks.'

So it wasn't very long before all the toys had fine new shoes and socks, better than their old ones, and they were very pleased indeed! But Amelia Jane wasn't pleased! She felt cross. She hadn't got any new shoes. It was too bad.

So what do you think she did? She took off her nice blue shoes, which were made of warm felt, and went to push them down the mouse-hole! But they were too big to go down, so Amelia Jane took them to the window, and threw them out! Perhaps they wouldn't be found – and then she too would have some new ones!

But, dear me, the two children were very cross with Amelia Jane when they found that her shoes were missing. 'You have lost them!' they said. 'You are getting very careless with your clothes, Amelia Jane. What you want is a good scolding.'

And they gave her such a scolding that she cried a puddle on to the floor. *What* a shock for naughty Amelia Jane!

But that wasn't the end of it. No – the children found her shoes out in the garden, where she had thrown them, wet through with the rain. They dried them and put them on Amelia's feet again. But they had shrunk smaller with the rain, and they were dreadfully tight. Really, poor

Amelia could hardly walk!

'I'm sorry I played about with your shoes,' Amelia Jane wept to the toys. 'I've been punished – and you've  all got nice new shoes – and *my* shoes are old and tight and hurt me! I'm very miserable.'

So the kind-hearted toys took off her shoes, and stretched them by pulling hard. Then they fitted Amelia Jane properly, and she dried her eyes and was very grateful.

'I won't play tricks again,' she said. 'I really won't.'

But nobody believed her – and I'm afraid I don't either!

It serves You Right, Amelia Jane

Once, when the children were away, there came such a fine sunny day that the toys longed to go out in the daytime, instead of waiting till night.

'I don't see why we shouldn't,' said the bear. 'There's no one about. Let's go and have a picnic in the orchard at the bottom of the garden.'

'Oh yes,' said Amelia Jane at once.

'Not *you*,' said the clown. 'You

don't behave yourself well enough. You can stay here. You're not asked to the picnic.'

'Well, I shall come all the same,' said Amelia, annoyed. 'So there!'

And she did. The toys couldn't stop her, for she was such a big, strong doll. She tossed her yellow hair in the air, smoothed down her red frock, and said 'Pooh!' whenever any toy said she was not to come.

'It's too bad!' said Tom the toy soldier, as he carried a basket of goodies down to the orchard. 'Amelia Jane has such a big appetite that she will eat far more than her share, and she's such a nuisance, always upsetting everyone and teasing them.'

'I wish
we could put her
somewhere that she couldn't get away
from,' said the clockwork mouse.
'She's taken my key away once
already today, and you know I won't
be able to go all the way down to the
orchard unless I'm wound up at least
twice.'

'It's a pity she couldn't climb a tree and not be able to get down!' said the bear. 'I've got some butterscotch for us to eat, and once Amelia sees it she will eat the lot!'

'I might be able to make her climb a tree,' said Tom suddenly, with a little giggle. 'Look, here's a fine place for a picnic, just under this old apple tree. Now, you watch me, and see if I don't get Amelia out of our way!'

The toys put down the baskets and packets they were carrying, and watched. Tom ran up to the tree and pretended to try to climb it. But he kept slipping back, and of course Amelia Jane laughed and laughed at him.

'Well, Amelia,' said Tom at last, 'you may laugh all you like, but *you* couldn't climb this tree either! It is very difficult. I did so want to get up it, because I hear you can see for miles around if you are at the top. But not even *you* could climb it!'

'Pooh!' said Amelia Jane at once. She was full of 'poohs' that day. 'I could easily climb it.'

'You couldn't,' said Tom.

'I could,' said Amelia.

'You couldn't!' cried everyone in glee, seeing the trick that the toy soldier was playing.

'Well, I'll just show

you, then!' cried Amelia, and she ran to the tree. But it really was rather difficult, because there was a big length of bare trunk before the branches began. Tom pushed Amelia up. All the toys came round and helped.

Whoosh! Amelia Jane shot up the trunk and came to where she could hold on to the branches. She was pleased that the toys were being so kind.

'Thank you!' she said. 'You are very helpful, Toys.'

'Don't mention it!' said Tom politely. 'We are pleased to push you up a tree.'

Amelia Jane began to climb up and up, feeling very proud. Ha, she could do what the other toys couldn't! She was a fine strong doll, and she would soon be at the top of the tree, and looking for miles around the country.

The toys took no more notice of her. They quickly undid their baskets and packets, sat down and began to enjoy their picnic in the green shade of the old apple tree. The sun lay in freckles of gold on the ground, and the clockwork mouse sat first on one freckle and then on another. It was fun.

'Hi, Toys, you're not watching me!' came Amelia Jane's voice suddenly from the top of the tree. 'Where are you? Look! I'm at the top of the tree! I can see such a lot of things.'

Nobody answered her. The toys grinned at one another, and Tom handed round some chocolate buns. The bear undid his packet of butterscotch. Everyone was very happy because naughty Amelia Jane wasn't there.

Amelia grew angry. She began to climb down the tree. She came to the lowest branches and peeped between the leaves. She saw the toys picnicking happily, and she was very angry.

'Toys! You've started without me! Oh, you mean things! I'm coming down at once!'

But she couldn't get down from the branches to the ground, for the jump was too big for her.

'Come and help me, Tom!' she

shouted. 'You pushed
me up – now you
can help me
down.'

The toy
soldier didn't
move. He took a bit
of butterscotch and
chewed it. It was lovely.

Amelia Jane was red
with rage.

'I shall miss the picnic!' she
cried. 'I shall miss the picnic.'

'You can't miss what you
haven't been asked to,' said
Tom, giggling.

'Eeee, eeee, eeee!'
laughed the clockwork
mouse.

'I want some butterscotch too!' squealed Amelia Jane.

'Well, go on wanting,' said the clown.

'Eeee, eeee, eeee!' laughed the mouse again. He thought it was all very funny.

'Oh, you mean things, you got me up this tree just to put me out of the way!' wept Amelia.

'Amelia Jane, you wanted to show how wonderful you were at climbing trees,' said Tom. 'Well, you've done what you wanted. And we've done what we wanted too! We've had a picnic without you. And now we are going to play games. Come on, Toys, let's play cowboys and indians.'

So they did, and hide-and-seek too, and

ball. Amelia Jane had to sit up on the branch of the apple tree and watch, and she didn't like it at all. She sulked and she cried.

'Cowboys and indians is a silly game!' she shouted rudely.

'Well, we're not asking *you* to play it!' said the clown.

'Eeee, eeee, eeee!' giggled the mouse.

'If that clockwork mouse giggles any more, I'll smack him!' said Amelia, weeping tears of rage.

'Come and smack me, then!' squealed the mouse, and he ran off, laughing.

Not until the toys were ready to go home again did they help Amelia Jane down. She was hungry and cross, and she felt rather ashamed of herself.

'Look, Amelia, we saved you a bun,' said the teddy bear, holding one out to her. 'We are sorry you were upset, but you shouldn't make yourself such a nuisance!'

'Thank you for the bun,' said Amelia in a small voice, and she ate it, though it was rather squashed, because the bear had sat on it by mistake.

'We'll ask you to our picnic next time, Amelia, if you'll be good,' said the toys.

'Well, I *will* be good then,' said

Amelia Jane. But I really don't think she can be!

Amelia Jane Gets a fright

Once Amelia Jane, the big naughty doll, thought it would be very funny to give everyone in the nursery a fright.

So she hid under the table behind the cushion, and when the sailor doll walked that way, she growled like a dog and pounced out at him.

It was dark under the table and the sailor doll really did think that there

was a dog there. He screamed and fled away to the toy-cupboard.

'What's the matter? What's the matter?' cried all the toys.

'There's a very fierce dog under the table,' said the sailor doll, shaking like a jelly. 'Or it might be a dragon. It was fierce enough.'

Amelia Jane nearly burst with trying not to laugh. She crouched down and hoped somebody else would come. Soon Tom the toy soldier came tiptoeing under the table, keeping a good look out for any fierce dog or dragon. Amelia Jane gave a deep growl.

Tom looked scared. He stopped.

'Urrrrr-grrrrr-urrrr!' said Amelia Jane, and she scrabbled at the floor as if she had claws.

'It's a dragon!' shouted Tom, and fled away so fast that he fell over the rug and went down on his nose. Amelia Jane let out a screech of laughter. The toys thought it was the howl of a dragon and they shivered in the cupboard.

Nobody would go under the table any more that night, and Amelia Jane

grew tired of hiding there. She thought she would play another trick on the toys, so she crept quietly out from under the table, climbed on to a chair, and took an apple from the dish of fruit there.

She sat on the table and scraped out two eyes in the apple and a big mouth.

She stuck a hazel nut hard into the apple for a nose. How funny it looked!

Amelia Jane laughed to herself, and crept down from the table with the apple-face. She found a pen with a sharp nib in the children's pencil-box and stuck the apple-face on to it. Then she crept round to the side of the toy-cupboard, where all the toys were sitting, listening for any sign of the dragon under the table.

Amelia Jane made a little squeaky noise. 'Eeeeee! Eeeeee! Eeeeeee!'

Everyone looked up. 'What was that?' said the teddy bear.

'It sounded like the clockwork mouse,' said the golden-haired doll.

'It wasn't, though,' said the clockwork mouse from his corner behind the brick-box. 'I'm here, and I didn't make a sound.'

'Eeee! Eeeee!' said Amelia Jane again, getting her apple-face on its pen-holder, so that she might stick it round the toy-cupboard door as soon as any toy peeped out.

'It's funny,' said the sailor doll. 'That's not a dragon. It sounded like a mouse or a bird or something.'

'I'll peep out and see,' said the teddy bear boldly. So he put his snout outside the cupboard door and tried to see what was squeaking.

And naughty Amelia Jane at once pushed her funny apple-face at the bear! How scared he was! He rushed back into the farthest corner of the toy-cupboard and squeezed down by the clockwork mouse.

'What was it?' cried all the toys.

'It was a face,' said the bear, trembling.

'A *face*!' said Tom scornfully. 'Well, what sort of a body had the face got?'

'It hadn't got a body,' said the bear. 'But it can't be a face,' said the sailor doll. 'I shall look.'

So he looked – and Amelia Jane

pushed her apple-face round the door
and made it jig up and down, so that
not only the sailor doll could see it but
everybody else could too!

'Go away!' cried Tom to the
apple-face. The apple-face grinned
widely, and jigged up and down
again peeping round the door. But
Amelia Jane knocked it by mistake
against the door and the hazel-nut
nose fell off!

The sailor doll picked up the nose
and found that it was only a nut! He
looked at the face and shouted: 'It's
just a silly apple-face, that's all! Don't
be scared, Toys – it's just a silly apple-
face!'

The toys rushed at the face and
pulled it off the penholder. They saw

Amelia Jane peeping round the corner, laughing till the tears ran down her cheeks, and they were very angry. Tom threw the apple-face at her, but Amelia dodged, and the apple knocked over a castle that the children had built of bricks. It fell with a crash.

'Sh! Sh!' said the bear. 'You'll wake the whole house up! Amelia Jane, how dare you frighten us all like that? Wasting a good apple too! I suppose you were the fierce dog or dragon under the table as well?'

'Yes,' said Amelia Jane, laughing all over her big face. 'Oh, it's such fun to frighten you, Toys. You are such a lot of sillies! Fancy being scared of an apple-face! I shall go on thinking of tricks to frighten you. It makes me laugh!'

The toys got in the toy-cupboard and shut the door. They were very angry with Amelia. They whispered about her, and tried to think how to stop her.

'If only we knew where she was every minute, we'd know it was Amelia and not dragons and things,' said Tom.

The clockwork mouse spoke up. 'Well, let's do something so that we always *do* know where Amelia Jane is!'

he said. 'There are some bells in the bead-box that came off the old reins. Couldn't the golden-haired doll sew them on to the under-hem of Amelia's skirt when she is asleep? Then wherever she went we should hear a little tinkling and know where she was!'

'Good idea!' said everyone, and they laughed. It was funny to think of Amelia Jane tinkling as she walked. They opened the door and peeped round it. Amelia Jane was sound asleep, tired out with all her tricks. Very quietly the golden-haired doll took the tiny bells from the bead-box and went up to Amelia Jane.

It didn't take a minute to sew two little bells on to the under-hem of her skirt. The golden-haired doll giggled and ran back to the cupboard.

And now it was no use Amelia Jane hiding anywhere to jump out at the toys, because they always heard the little tinkle that told them where she was! So Amelia didn't manage to give anyone a scare at all for the next few nights, and she was cross.

She couldn't *think* where the tinkle came from – but at last she found the little bells. She *was* angry! She pulled them off her skirt, and then she pinned them to the curtain by the window. Every time the wind blew the curtain the bells tinkled!

'Amelia Jane is behind the curtain!' whispered the toys to one another. But she wasn't! It was only the bells tinkling there. Amelia was hiding in the cupboard, meaning to jump at the toys when they came in. And what a fright she gave them!

'She's taken off her bells!' cried Tom. 'We must think of something else!'

They hustled Amelia Jane out of their cupboard and slammed the door. Amelia laughed and climbed into the dolls' cot. The dolls were not there. They were in the toy-cupboard, talking.

'Well, they won't be able to sleep *here* tonight!' said Amelia, and she snuggled down comfortably and went to sleep.

'You know,' said Tom to the toys in the cupboard, 'there's only one thing to do to stop Amelia Jane from scaring us. And that's to scare *her*!'

'Let's!' shouted the toys.

'But how?' asked the bear.

'There are a lot of brown stockings in the dolls' trunk,' said Tom, grinning. 'What about getting them out, sewing them neatly together, and pretending they are a long snake?'

'But how will that frighten Amelia Jane?' asked the sailor doll.

'Well, we'll pin the stocking-snake on to the back of her shoe,' grinned

Tom. 'Then we'll say there's a snake after her – and no matter how she runs away from it, it will follow her because it will be fastened to her! Don't you remember how she once put a plasticine tail on to the bear?'

'Oh, good!' said the toys. They ran to get the brown stockings. The golden-haired doll sewed them neatly together till they looked like a wriggly brown snake. Then she tiptoed to the cot where Amelia Jane lay asleep. She pinned the stocking-snake to the back of Amelia's shoe.

'Now we must all make a noise and shout out that there is a snake loose in the nursery!' said Tom. 'We must pretend we are very frightened.'

So they began to shout and make

a noise. 'Ooh, a snake! Look out, a
snake! A snake!'

Amelia Jane woke and sat up.
She was afraid of snakes.

'Where is it?' she cried.

'We think it went into your cot!'
shouted the toys. 'Look! There it is
in your cot, Amelia! Run!'

Amelia screamed and jumped from
the cot, but as the stocking-snake was
pinned to the back of her shoe, it had
to come after her wherever she
went! Oh dear!
how Amelia
screamed and
ran and
dodged! It
wasn't a bit of
use, the snake

went wherever she did!

'It's biting my foot, it's biting my foot!' she squealed. 'Save me, Toys, save me!'

But the toys were laughing too much to do anything. Amelia ran and ran. 'Go away, you horrid snake! Go after the others! Oh, Toys, save me, and I promise never to scare you again!'

'Do you mean that promise?' asked the teddy bear at once. 'Very well – I will save you from the snake – though it would have served you right if it had eaten you up.'

He ran to Amelia and undid the pin. Then he waved the stocking-snake in her face.

'You made an apple-face – and we

made a stocking-snake!' he said. 'Ho, ho, Amelia Jane, it *was* fun to see you running away from a row of brown stockings!'

Amelia was angry. She stalked off to the dolls' cot again and didn't say another word. But the toys said plenty – and how they did laugh! Amelia wouldn't scare them again in a hurry!

Amelia Jane in the Country

Now you remember that the toys told Amelia Jane she could come with them to their next picnic if she was good, don't you? Well, the big doll managed to be fairly good for a few days – and then the teddy bear thought it would be fine to go for a day in the country.

'Can I come too?' asked Amelia Jane.

'You haven't been *very* good,' said the bear, rather sternly.

'Well, I haven't been very bad either,' said Amelia. 'I've only put salt in your tea once, instead of sugar – and I've not taken away the mouse's key at all.'

'Yes, but you have kicked a marble up into the air and made it fall into my jug of milk at teatime,' said Tom the toy soldier.

'I couldn't help that,' said Amelia. 'I didn't know you were going to put your milk on the table just then.'

'Well, don't let's quarrel,' said the clown. 'She can come if she doesn't do anything silly. How shall we go? It's a long way to the country.'

'The wooden train will take some

of us, and the bus too, and the motor-car can take two or three,' said Tom. So it was all arranged. The golden-haired doll did some cooking on the stove, and made buns and biscuits. Tom took an apple from the fruit-dish. If he cut it up into slices there would be plenty for everyone.

They got into the train, the car, and the bus. There was just room for everyone, though Amelia Jane had to ride on the boiler of the engine because she was so big! She didn't mind that – she thought it was fun.

'I'm going to take my butterfly-net with me,' she said, just before they started. 'I might be able to catch some butterflies.'

'No, don't do that,' said Tom. 'It isn't kind to catch the pretty things. Leave your net behind.'

But Amelia Jane wouldn't. She stuck it down the funnel of the engine and off they went, the butterfly-net looking most peculiar waggling about in the funnel!

It was lovely out in the country. The sun shone, the daisies smiled everywhere, and the bees hummed like tiny aeroplanes. Amelia Jane was so happy that she went quite mad! She ran all over the place, shouting and laughing. She took her butterfly-net and began to try to catch the big white butterflies that flew everywhere.

But the butterflies wouldn't be caught! Not one of those white ones could Amelia catch. So she hunted the little blue ones – but they were very nimble and soared high into the air long before Amelia could get her net down on them.

'Amelia Jane, do stop rushing about trying to catch butterflies that won't be caught,' said Tom. 'You make me feel quite hot, watching you tear about.'

'Well, don't watch then,' said Amelia, racing after a red-and-black butterfly.

'Look, Amelia, that's a Red Admiral!' said the bear, proud of

knowing the butterfly's name. But
Amelia didn't know he was talking
about a butterfly. She thought he
meant a red sailor – a real admiral!
She looked all around for him.

'And there goes a Painted Lady!'
cried the bear proudly, as a pretty,
gaily coloured butterfly fluttered past.
'Oh, and there's a Peacock! You can't
catch those, Amelia Jane!'

'Of course I can't catch a red
sailor or a lady or a peacock bird!'
cried Amelia Jane. 'Don't be silly! But
where's the famous sailor, Teddy
Bear? I can't see an admiral
anywhere. And where's the lady, all
painted up? I can't see her either. And
I'm sure there isn't a lovely peacock
about, showing off its beautiful tail!'

The toys squealed with laughter. 'She thinks they are real people and birds!' giggled the sailor doll. 'She doesn't know they are only names of pretty butterflies. Silly Amelia Jane!'

Well, if there was one thing that Amelia hated, it was being called silly. She lost her temper and rushed at the toys.

'I can't catch admirals and ladies and peacocks,' she said, 'but I'll catch a sailor and a doll and a mouse. So there!'

She brought her butterfly-net down over the surprised sailor doll, and there he was, caught! Amelia Jane laughed with delight. She twisted the net over, and there was the sailor doll bobbing about, terribly afraid of falling out.

Amelia tipped him out, bump!

What a bruise he got! Then the naughty doll ran to catch the golden-haired doll, who swallowed a crumb down the wrong way in alarm and began to choke. Amelia caught her up neatly in her net. She swung her up in the air and tipped her out, bump!

'I'm catching butterflies, I'm catching butterflies!' sang Amelia Jane joyfully. She ran after the clockwork mouse, who scuttled away at once. But his clockwork soon ran down and Amelia caught him up. Up he went in the net – and down he came, bump! His key was knocked out and flew off into the grass. The sailor at once went to hunt for it, because if it was lost the mouse would never be able to run again.

'Amelia Jane, stop!' shouted all the toys in a rage. 'Stop!'

'I'm catching butterflies, I'm catching butterflies!' sang Amelia, and she caught all the toys with her long net, one after another, tipping them out, bump, as soon as she had swung them up into the air! Oh, she was behaving very badly indeed!

'We'll never, never trust you again, Amelia Jane,' said the teddy bear angrily. 'We'll never speak to you again. You've spoilt the picnic. You are a tiresome, naughty doll, and we shall leave you behind here. We don't want you ever to come back to the nursery again!'

They climbed into the train, the car, and the bus. They wouldn't let Amelia Jane ride on the engine boiler as she had when they came. They pushed her off. They wouldn't let her ride with them at all.

'But I shall be lost all by myself here,' wept Amelia, really frightened.

'Don't leave me behind.'

'Amelia Jane, this time we mean what we say,' said Tom, starting the engine. 'We don't want you, and we don't care what becomes of you. Goodbye!'

And off they started, chuff-chuff-chuff-r-r-r-r-r, rumble-umble-umble! Amelia Jane watched them go, and she wept bitterly, for she knew that she could never find her way back to the nursery alone.

But, oh dear – a dreadful thing happened! The train somehow took the wrong path. It took the path that led to the river – and do you know, before it could stop itself it had run right into the water – splash!

Into the river went the toys,

struggling and splashing. The little
duck could swim, but no one else.
They began to shout and splutter.
'Help! Help! Help!'

Now the car and bus had managed
to stop in time, and the toys inside
them ran to help the others.

But they couldn't reach them.

Whatever were they to do? Everyone began to shout and sob and cry.

Amelia Jane heard the noise, for the engine had not gone very far before it fell into the river. The big doll listened in surprise. What was happening? She dried her tears and set off to see. When she turned the corner she stared in astonishment and fright. The golden-haired doll was struggling in the river, and the pink rabbit, and the clockwork mouse! Tom was there too, sinking for the third time.

Now Amelia was naughty but she wasn't bad, and as soon as she saw that dreadful sight she was as upset as the rest of the toys. She rushed to the river at once, shouting,

'Save them, save them!'

'We can't!' wept the toys. 'We can't reach!'

And then Amelia Jane had a wonderful idea. 'My butterfly-net!' she cried. 'My net! I can catch them like fish!'

She stood on the bank and put her big net into the river. She slipped it under the toy soldier. She caught him and dragged him to the shore. She tipped him out safely and then put her net in again. She caught the golden-haired doll, and dragged her out, dripping wet.

Then she fished for the pink rabbit and the clockwork mouse, and caught them both together. Out they came, gasping and spluttering, on to the bank.

'Oh, Amelia, thank you!' cried the toys, hugging her. 'Oh, you've saved them all! We *are* glad you brought your net with you, even though you caught us like butterflies. But it's been so useful, and you've been so good! Oh, Amelia, you are so very naughty and so very good too!'

'Can I go back to the nursery with you, please?' asked Amelia Jane humbly.

'Of course, of course!' cried the toys. 'Get on to the boiler of the engine, Amelia. You shall drive. We must hurry back and dry the poor wet toys, or they will get dreadful colds. Hurry, hurry!'

So off they all went back to the nursery again, and Amelia Jane's butterfly-net was stuck, dripping wet, into the funnel, where it looked even more peculiar than before. But nobody minded. And Amelia Jane was very happy. She had been good and the toys loved her after all. She really did feel pleased!

Amelia Jane
and the Pig

Once, when naughty Amelia Jane was
poking about in the toy-cupboard,
she found an old balloon-pig, quite
flat.

You've seen those balloon-pigs,
haven't you? You blow them up like
balloons, and they stand on four
funny little legs, have a squiggly tail
and a nose that you blow into to
make the pig fat. And when they go

down they make a dreadful wailing noise.

Well, as soon as Amelia Jane saw that balloon-pig, she was *very* pleased! Now she could play a fine trick on the toys.

'I shall make them jump like anything!' she said. 'Oh, won't they be frightened! The toy soldier will run away, and the clown will hide under a chair!'

Amelia Jane took the pig to the dolls' house. There was nobody there. All the toys were looking at a book at the other end of the nursery.

Amelia pushed the pig in through the little front door. It was still flat, so it went in quite easily. Then she put her mouth to its nose and blew.

She blew and blew. The pig grew fat. The air inside it blew up its round little body, and it became like a proper little pig. It stood on its four legs. Its tail stood up nicely. Its tiny, painted eyes looked at Amelia in surprise.

Amelia Jane grinned at the pig. 'You're going to give everyone a dreadful scare when you go down flat!' she said. 'Now mind you squeal and wail at the top of your voice!'

The pig stared at her. It didn't want to go down flat. It liked being a fat, round pig.

Amelia took her thumb away from the pig's snout. Air began to escape from it at once – and the pig began to make that strange wailing noise that all balloon-pigs make.

'Eeeee-oooow-eeeee, oooooo-ooh!'
What a dreadful noise it made!

Amelia Jane hid inside the toy-cupboard and watched what would happen. The clockwork clown fell down flat with surprise. Tom ran away and fell over a brick, bang! on to his nose. The clockwork mouse shot into the golden-haired doll and upset her on the floor. What a disturbance there was!

'What's that? What's that?' cried the teddy bear, looking all round. 'Somebody's in trouble! Somebody is wailing for help! Quick, quick, what is it?'

'Perhaps it's Amelia Jane making that awful noise,' said the clown, looking round.

Amelia Jane stuck her head out of the toy-cupboard. 'Well, it's not me!' she said. 'It must be the Tiddley-Widdley-Wonkies! They always make a noise like that!'

The toys had never heard of the Tiddley-Widdley-Wonkies before – and no wonder, because Amelia Jane had made the name up just that very minute. The toys looked at one another in horror.

'The Tiddley-Widdley-Wonkies!'
said the teddy bear. 'What are they?
Why do they make that awful noise?'

'Eeeeeee-oooooo-ow-ooooo-eeeeh!'
wailed the balloon-pig in the dolls'
house. The toys clutched one another
and went pale. This was dreadful.

'Will the Tiddley-Widdley-
Wonkies eat us?' asked the poor little
clockwork mouse, trembling so much
that his tail shook like a catkin on a
tree.

'Oh, of course, if they get you!'
said Amelia Jane, enjoying herself
very much. 'Look out! They may
come for you any minute!'

'Eeeee-oooo-ow-ooooooh!'
wailed the pig, slowly getting
flatter as he squealed. The toys

rushed to the toy-cupboard and clambered in, trembling.

'I d-d-d-don't like the Tiddley-Widdley-Wonkies,' wept the clockwork mouse, who was always easily frightened.

'Well, I'll tell them to go, then,' said Amelia Jane grandly.

She knew that the pig must be almost flat by now, and would soon stop squealing. So she went out of the cupboard and called loudly: 'Tiddley-Widdley-Wonkies! Go away at once, or I, Amelia Jane, will come after you and get you!'

'Eeeeeeeeeeeeeeeeh!' said the pig in the dolls' house, and then said no more. He was quite flat now – not a scrap of air was left inside him.

There was silence. 'There you are!'
said Amelia Jane. 'The Tiddley-
Widdley-Wonkies are afraid of me.
They've gone!'

'Oh, thank you, Amelia Jane!'
cried all the toys. 'That *was* brave of
you!'

Amelia Jane giggled away to
herself all that night, whenever she
thought of the squealing pig. She
made up her naughty little mind to
play the same trick again the very
next night.

So when she saw that the toys were
busy playing at the other end of the
nursery, she went over to the dolls'
house again, and put her hand in at
the window to pick up the flat
balloon-pig. She got hold of his nose

and began to blow air into him.

Now the clockwork mouse happened to be in the dolls' house that night. He had curled himself up in one of the cots there, as he sometimes did when he was tired. But Amelia Jane didn't know that. He was in the bedroom just above the room where the balloon-pig was.

Well, Amelia Jane blew and blew till the balloon-pig was fat. Then she ran off to the toy-cupboard again and listened to the pig beginning to wail, 'Eeeeeeeee-ooooooh!'

'It's the Tiddley-Widdley-Wonkies again!' yelled the clown. 'Come on and hide, everybody!'

They ran to hide, and then found that the clockwork mouse was not with them. Where was he?

Well, he was in the dolls' house as you know – and, dear me, how frightened he was when he heard that dreadful wailing noise in the room below him! He jumped out of the cot, and ran downstairs to escape.

But he couldn't escape because the balloon-pig was so fat and big that he blocked the front door. The mouse couldn't get out, and he was just about to run back upstairs in fright, when he saw that it was the pig who was making the noise.

'It's not the Tiddley-Widdley-Wonkies then!' said the mouse to himself. 'It's just that old balloon-pig, and I guess it's Amelia Jane who's blown him up, too, just to give us a fright – the bad doll!'

The clockwork mouse found a pin that was pinning up the curtains. He dug it into the balloon-pig.

Pop! The pig burst.

'I've killed the Tiddley-Widdley-Wonkies! I've killed the Tiddley-Widdley-Wonkies!' cried the little mouse, rushing out of the front door in delight.

'What! What! How did you do it?' cried all the toys, running up.

Proudly the mouse showed them the flat pig.

The toys stared and stared.

'That's Amelia Jane again,' said the clown in a rage. 'Frightening us all like that!'

'Let's give *her* a scare too,' said the bear. 'Can't we think of something that will make a noise and frighten her dreadfully? It's just no good letting her do these things to us.'

'Well, what noise can we make?' said the golden-haired doll. They all thought hard.

'If I rub my paw hard against the window-pane it makes a fine squeaky noise,' said the bear.

'And if I get the slate out of the cupboard and press hard on it with a pencil, it makes a terrible squeal,' said Tom, grinning.

'And if I get that old broken violin out of the chest there, and pull its one string, it goes "Plooonk! Ploooonk!"

just like that,' said the clown. 'I saw one of the children doing it the other day.'

'Well, we'll do all that,' said the doll, pleased. So the clown went to get the old violin. It still had just one string. The clown hid it behind the coal-scuttle, and waited there.

The teddy bear climbed up to the window-sill and hid behind the curtain. Tom got the old slate out of the cupboard, found a broken slate-pencil, and hid it under the table behind the cushion there.

Now they would wait until Amelia came by.

Amelia was looking at the pig in the dolls' house, wondering if she could mend him. She felt very angry

with the mouse for spoiling her joke.
The mouse watched her. It was his job
to make Amelia Jane run near the
coal-scuttle, the window, and the
table if he could so that the toys could
make their noises.

'You wait till I catch you, you
naughty little mouse!' cried Amelia.

'Can't catch me, can't catch me!'
squeaked the mouse joyfully, and ran
off. Amelia Jane ran after him. He ran
by the window. The teddy bear ran
his paw up and down at once.
'Eeeeeeh! Eeeeeeeh! Eeeeeeh!'

'Oh! what's that?' cried Amelia in
a fright. She ran under the table – but
Tom was waiting there with his slate
and pencil. He rubbed the pencil hard
up and down the slate. What a

terrible squealing it made! Amelia jumped as if she had been shot, and ran straight into the table-leg, bump!

'Ow-ee, ow-ee, ow-ee!' went the slate pencil. Amelia Jane rushed away, and saw the mouse grinning at her from behind the coal-scuttle. She ran after him in a great rage. She didn't know that the clown was there with the old violin! He pulled the string a good many times.

'Ploooonk! Plooonk! Plooooonk!' growled the violin.

'Oh! Who's hiding there? Who's growling at me?' yelled poor Amelia.

'It's the Tiddley-Widdley-Wonkies, of course,' shouted all the toys in delight. 'Look out, Amelia Jane, look out!'

Amelia Jane rushed into the cupboard, shut the door, and shivered. Were there really Tiddley-Widdley-Wonkies after all? Oh dear, oh dear, oh dear!

And there she stayed for two whole nights and wouldn't go out to play! Poor Amelia Jane!

Amelia Jane is Terribly Naughty

Once Amelia Jane, the big naughty doll, discovered a tiny hole in the quilt on the dolls' cot. So she poked her finger inside and pulled out a feather. She threw it up into the air.

'Look!' she shouted. 'This quilt is full of feathers. Did you know there were feathers in quilts, Toys?'

'Amelia Jane! Don't pull out any more feathers!' said Tom at once,

276

seeing the big doll pull out two more.

'Oh, I must, I must,' said Amelia, and she tore the hole a little more till it was quite a big one. Then she could put in her hand – and out came dozens of feathers!

'I shall make a snowstorm, a snowstorm, a snowstorm!' sang Amelia Jane in delight. She climbed up on to the nursery table and began to shake the quilt. Well, as you can imagine, out flew hundreds and hundreds of white feathers! Amelia Jane became very excited.

'I'm making snow, I'm making snow!' she shouted. 'Come out in the snowstorm, Toys!'

The toys stared at the naughty doll in dismay. What a mess she was

making! Whatever were they to do?

The feathers flew all about the room, floating lightly in the air, and it really did look rather like a snowstorm.

Amelia Jane got another quilt – and she made a hole at one end.

She climbed up to the table again and shook the quilt. Out flew hundreds more feathers!

She squealed with delight.

'You'll soon be able to make a snow-
man, Toys!'

'Don't be silly, Amelia Jane,' said
the clockwork clown. 'I simply can't
think how you can be so naughty.'

'Oh, it's quite easy,' said bad
Amelia Jane, and she shook twenty
feathers down on to the clockwork
clown's head. The clockwork mouse
watched from a corner. He really felt
a bit afraid of so many feathers.

'I wonder where there is another
quilt,' said Amelia Jane, who never
could stop, once she had begun. 'Oh,
I believe I know where there is
an old cushion. That will be full of
feathers too. I think I saw one of
the children put it on the top shelf
of the nursery cupboard. I'll climb

up and see.'

She went to the cupboard, walking through the cloud of feathers. She blew them away as she went. It was fun. She came to the cupboard and opened the door. In the cupboard were many shelves, for a great deal was kept there – the nursery cups and saucers were there, the knives and forks, the treacle for the porridge, the honey, the jam, a tin of biscuits, mending things – and on the top shelf was a collection of things that needed sewing – a cushion with a hole in, a teacloth, and a tablecloth.

Amelia Jane began to climb up the shelves – and then a dreadful thing happened. She caught hold of the saucer in which the tin of treacle stood

– and it tipped up at once. The lid came off – the treacle tin lost its balance and fell straight on Amelia Jane's head. The treacle trickled down all over her.

'Ooooh, Amelia Jane! Now look what you've done,' shouted the toys, as they saw the treacle dripping down all over the big doll.

'Oh, I don't like it! It's sticky!' cried Amelia Jane, and she jumped down from the cupboard.

And then a funny thing happened.
The feathers, which were still floating
all over the room, fell on to the sticky
treacle – and before you could say,
'Look at Amelia Jane!' she was
covered with feathers!

The toys began to laugh. They
simply couldn't help it.
First Amelia was
covered with treacle,
and then with
feathers – and
it was all
because of her
own naughtiness!

'*Don't* laugh
at me, you horrid
things!' yelled Amelia
in a temper, and she

ran at the toys. But the more she ran through the feathers, the more they stuck to her – and at last she looked like a strange and peculiar bird!

The toys laughed till they couldn't laugh any more. Amelia Jane got angrier and angrier, and tried to tear off the feathers. Then she lay down on the floor and rolled about to get them off – but she forgot that there were hundreds of feathers on the carpet, so when she got up there were more stuck to her than ever!

'It's the funniest sight I've ever seen,' said Tom, wiping his eyes, for he had laughed till he cried. Amelia Jane flew at the toy soldier. Then she ran at the teddy bear and the frightened clockwork mouse. She was a big doll and the toys were really terrified, but Amelia wouldn't stop.

'*I'll* teach you to laugh at me!' she cried.

And then something happened to Amelia. The door of the nursery opened softly, and in walked the big black kitchen cat. When he saw Amelia Jane covered in feathers, he stopped and stared.

'What! A *bird* in the nursery!' he mewed. 'I'll catch it for my dinner!'

Then it was Amelia's turn to be frightened. She ran into a corner and hid there. 'No, don't catch me, don't catch me!' she cried. 'I'm Amelia Jane!'

'Rubbish!' said the cat. 'You've got feathers growing on you – dolls don't

have feathers! I shall catch you, you
most peculiar bird!'

He crept quietly up to the corner.
Amelia gave a squeal and ran away.
She hid behind the brick-box. The cat
followed again, and crouched down,
ready to spring. Amelia yelled for
help.

'Toys! Save me! Save me! Quick,
come and help me!'

But the toys thought it was time
that Amelia was punished. Now she
must see what it was like to be chased
and hurt.

The cat sprang. He landed right
on Amelia Jane and squashed all the
breath out of her. He dug his claws
into her and scratched her. She
squealed and squealed.

He sniffed at her in disgust and then jumped away. He couldn't bear the sticky treacle on his paws. He licked them clean and then walked out of the nursery with his tail in the air.

'You're only a doll after all,' he said. 'Well, if you dress yourself up in feathers and treacle, you must expect trouble!'

Amelia Jane cried so much that the toys came round to comfort her. She had had her punishment, and they were too kind-hearted to keep away any longer.

'Now listen to me, Amelia,' said Tom sternly. 'We will wash the treacle off you – but after that you must see to the feathers. You must pick up every single one and stuff them all back into the quilts, and sew up the holes. Do you hear?'

'Yes, Tom,' said Amelia Jane in a small voice. So they took her to the basin and washed away the treacle. It made her very wet and she had to dry herself by the fire. Then she had to pick up all the feathers. Nobody helped her, because, as the toy soldier said, she really had to learn that she must pay for being naughty.

Then Amelia Jane put the feathers back and sewed up the holes in the quilts. 'I've done all you said,' she said in a sorry sort of voice. 'I won't be bad again.'

But nobody believed her – and I don't expect you do either!

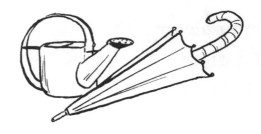

Amelia Jane is Tired

Once Amelia Jane, the big naughty doll, went out walking with the teddy bear. They went to the shops and Amelia Jane spent fifty pence. She bought a little watering-can, and the teddy bear wasn't at all pleased.

'I suppose you'll use that to water the toys, instead of watering flowers,' he said. 'Well – I shall buy something really sensible. I want an umbrella.'

'An *umbrella*!' said Amelia Jane with a giggle. 'What do you want an umbrella for?'

'Well, it might rain, mightn't it?' said the teddy bear, in a huff.

'There isn't a cloud in the sky and the sun is shining brightly,' said Amelia Jane. 'But still, if you think it will rain out of a blue sky, you'd certainly better buy the umbrella, Teddy.'

The bear had seen a really lovely umbrella. It was bright red, and had a beautiful handle made of red glass. The bear asked how much it was, and was very delighted when he found that he had enough money to pay for it.

He bought it, and proudly set off

home with it. It really looked very nice indeed. Amelia Jane half wished *she* had bought an umbrella too. But still, she liked her green watering-can, and planned all sorts of tricks with it.

They lost their way and walked about a mile before they came to a place they knew. Amelia Jane felt tired. She told the bear.

'Teddy, please give me a piggy-back home,' she said. 'I'm too tired to walk any further.'

'Well! I like *that*!' said the bear, surprised. 'Give you a piggy-back home when I'm very tired myself? I should think not indeed! You can walk home on your own feet.'

'Oh, *do* give me a piggy-back,' begged Amelia. But the bear said no, and no, and no. Three times he said it, each time more loudly than the last. Then he sat down below a tree and yawned.

'I must just have a rest,' he said. 'Sit quietly, now, Amelia. Don't disturb me.'

Amelia Jane frowned at the bear. Then, when she saw that he had shut his eyes, she smiled. She stole off to a little stream nearby and filled her green watering-can. Then she quietly climbed the tree above the teddy bear and sat on a low-hanging branch there, hidden in the leaves.

She tipped up the can. A shower of little cold drops went down on the bear. He opened his eyes in a hurry.

'Amelia! Oh, Amelia, it's

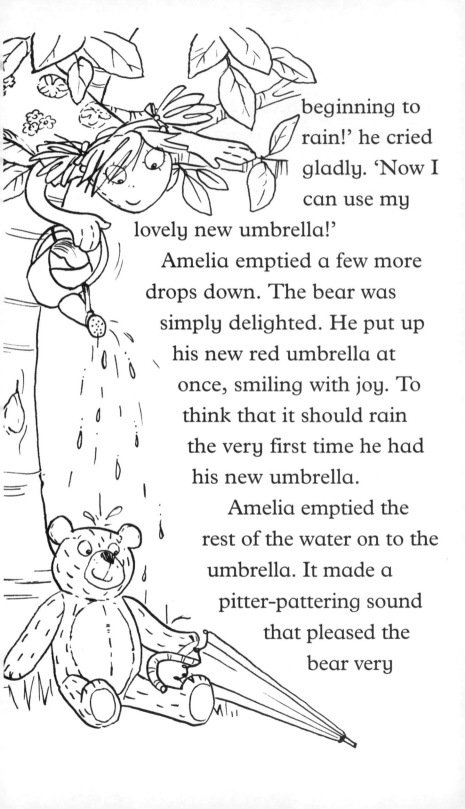

beginning to rain!' he cried gladly. 'Now I can use my lovely new umbrella!'

Amelia emptied a few more drops down. The bear was simply delighted. He put up his new red umbrella at once, smiling with joy. To think that it should rain the very first time he had his new umbrella.

Amelia emptied the rest of the water on to the umbrella. It made a pitter-pattering sound that pleased the bear very much. He listened to it, with his head on one side.

Amelia carefully let herself down from the tree-branch and sat on top of the red umbrella, holding on to the little stick that stuck up from the bottom. The bear didn't know anything about Amelia doing this, for he couldn't see through the umbrella!

He thought that his umbrella was very heavy, though. Still, that made him rather proud.

That's the umbrella getting wet, I suppose, he thought. The rain is wetting it and making it heavy. What a fine umbrella it is. Then he looked round for Amelia.

'Amelia Jane! Where are you? I'm going home. You can share my umbrella with me if you like, so that you don't get wet.'

Amelia Jane grinned. She was sharing the umbrella all right – and she wasn't getting wet either! She didn't say a word.

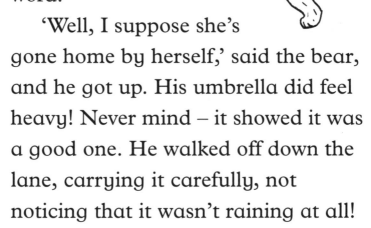

'Well, I suppose she's gone home by herself,' said the bear, and he got up. His umbrella did feel heavy! Never mind – it showed it was a good one. He walked off down the lane, carrying it carefully, not noticing that it wasn't raining at all!

He got back to the nursery, and the toys were *most* surprised to see the umbrella up – with Amelia Jane on top of it! They crowded round in astonishment.

'Hallo!' said the bear. 'See my new umbrella? Isn't it fine? Is Amelia Jane home yet? Do you know, she wanted me to *carry* her home! I said no, no, NO. As if I would dream of carrying that great fat doll home. The idea!'

The toys giggled. The bear frowned at them. 'What are you giggling at?' he asked. 'Surely you are not giggling at my fine new umbrella?'

'No – we are giggling because you said you wouldn't carry Amelia Jane home – and you have!' laughed the clockwork clown.

'I have not,' said the bear crossly.

'You have!' cried Amelia Jane, and she thumped on the top of the umbrella. 'I'm here!'

The bear let down his umbrella at once – and Amelia Jane slipped to the ground as it shut. The bear stared at her in a rage, and Amelia Jane stared back.

'You bad doll,' said the bear. 'No wonder my umbrella felt heavy. You might have broken it. How dare you make me carry you when I said I wouldn't!'

'Oh, I like getting my own way,' said Amelia Jane, and she laughed and laughed.

But then she found that she had left behind her nice little new watering-can! She had left it in the tree. She *was* upset. 'Oh, please, will someone go back and fetch it for me?' she cried.

But nobody would. 'What! Fetch a watering-can that you only bought because you thought you could play tricks on us with it!' cried the sailor doll. 'I should think not indeed. We'll leave the can there for somebody else to find – and serve you right too, Amelia Jane!'

So the little green can is still up the tree, and nobody has found it yet. Wouldn't it be fun if *you* did!

A Shock for Amelia Jane

Amelia Jane had no manners at all. She was the biggest doll in the nursery, and you might have thought she would be the best behaved. But she wasn't.

Whenever other toys paid a visit to the nursery they were always shocked by Amelia Jane. She never shook hands and said how-do-you-do. She never said goodbye nicely. And she never offered visiting toys any sweets, even if she had some.

So you can guess that the toys who lived with Amelia Jane were ashamed of her.

'When Peter brought his toy soldier the other day, Amelia Jane squirted him with the water pistol,' said the clockwork clown.

'And when Betsy-May brought her best doll for a visit, Amelia Jane dabbed her with a paint-brush and made her nose all blue,' said the teddy bear.

'Yes, but the worst thing she ever did was to make a hole in that floating duck that Billy-Bob brought to show our children,' said the clockwork mouse. 'She poked it with a pin – and it filled with water and sank. That was a very bad thing to do.'

'I wish we could teach her manners,' said the teddy bear.

'So do I,' said the golden-haired doll, who had most beautiful manners herself, and always said 'thank you' and 'please' at the right moments.

The clockwork mouse began to giggle. He had a funny giggle that went on and on, and it made the other toys giggle too.

'What's the matter?' asked Tom.

'I've got a little idea,' said the mouse, quivering his rubber tail. 'Can't we dress something up, and pretend it is someone come to see if we've got manners, and give Amelia Jane a shock?'

'But what could we dress up?' asked the golden-haired doll. 'I don't see what you mean.'

'Well, listen,' said the clockwork mouse. 'You know that balloon in the cupboard, don't you? Let's paint a face on it, and stick some hairs on, and put a hat on it. Then one of us could wrap a coat and a shawl round our shoulders and head and pretend that the balloon-face is our face – and we could come visiting the nursery and pretend to be very shocked at Amelia's manners.'

'Yes – it might be a good idea,' said the clown. 'It would certainly be

very funny. We'll try it! And oh, I say!
We'll tell Amelia Jane that it's Mrs
Good-Manners come to visit us, and
that she'll burst with rage if she finds
any of us without good manners –
and we'll stick a pin into her head at
the back when Amelia is being rude to
her, to make her really burst. Oh,
what a shock for Amelia Jane!'

The toys began to giggle again.
Amelia Jane had gone out in the pram
with the children, so they had plenty
of time to do what they wanted to.
The clown ran to the cupboard and

took out the
balloon. He
blew it up till it
was nice and
round.

The teddy bear got the paint-box and painted rather a fierce sort of face on the balloon. Tom begged the rocking-horse for some hairs out of his tail and stuck them on to the balloon-face for hair. Then the toys found an old doll's hat with flowers in, and put that on the balloon-head. It did look funny.

'*I'll* be Mrs Good-Manners,' said the teddy bear, who was nice and plump. He giggled. 'This is going to be funny. I shall love being Mrs Good-Manners! Get me an old dress and a shawl, and some doll's boots for my feet.'

Very soon the bear was all dressed up, and the toys tied the balloon-neck to the shawl that went over his head. He really looked as if the balloon-face was his own face – it was very funny.

The bear put on a most polite kind of voice and walked round the nursery curtseying and bowing to everyone.

'Good-day! *Good*-day! I hope I see you well? And how do you do, *dear* Mister Clockwork Clown? How is your dear mother? Oh, and here is *dear* little Clockwork Mouse. How are you, my pet?'

Everyone squealed with laughter to see the big balloon-face with its old hat on top, waggling round at everyone as the bear trotted about the nursery. The mouse couldn't say a word because he was laughing so much. Even his tail seemed to laugh and got all curled up.

'Oh, you're lovely, Teddy!' cried Tom. 'Now listen – you act just like this when Amelia Jane comes, won't you – and be very, very shocked if she's rude – and after a bit I'll creep behind you with a pin and dig it into your balloon-head without Amelia noticing. And then what a shock she will get!'

Just then the children came back, and Amelia Jane was with them. The toys scurried into the toy-cupboard – all except the bear, and he slipped out into the passage and hid in the broom-cupboard there.

Well, when the nursery was empty again, and the children had gone to their rest, there came a knock at the door.

'Who's that?' said Amelia in surprise.

'I think it's Mrs Good-Manners come to pay us a visit,' said Tom. 'I did hear she was going round the nurseries to make sure that toys knew their manners.'

'Oh, really?' said Amelia in surprise. 'What a silly person she must be! *I* shan't be polite to her.'

'You must be, Amelia Jane,' said Tom. 'She may be very cross if you are not.'

The knocking came again. The clown went across the nursery and opened the door. In walked the bear, dressed up as Mrs Good-Manners, with his balloon-head waggling about.

'Good-day!' said Mrs Good-Manners, going across to the clockwork clown. 'And how do you do?'

'Very well, thank you,' answered the clown politely, 'and how are you?'

'Well, I thank you,' answered Mrs Good-Manners. Then she turned to Amelia Jane and held out her hand.

'And how are you, Amelia Jane?' she asked.

'Oh, I've got earache in my toes and toothache in my knee,' said Amelia very rudely, and she wouldn't shake hands.

'What bad manners!' said Mrs

Good-Manners, shocked. 'You make me feel quite faint.'

'I'll throw some cold water over you then. That will make you feel better!' said Amelia Jane.

'Pray do no such thing,' said Mrs Good-Manners hurriedly. 'Amelia, you are a very rude doll. I must insist that you learn better manners.'

'Insist all you like,' said Amelia rudely. 'I think good manners are just silly. Now do go away. We don't want you in our nursery!'

'Amelia Jane, you are making me very cross!' said Mrs Good-Manners in a fierce voice, and her head waggled about in a rather alarming manner. Amelia felt a little uncomfortable. She had never seen anyone with such a waggly head before.

'Oh, go away!' said the naughty doll. 'I'm tired of you!'

'Amelia! You will make Mrs Good-Manners burst with rage!' cried Tom, running up. 'Be careful! She is getting angrier and angrier.'

'*She* won't burst with rage!' said Amelia. 'People never do!'

'I'm going to burst! I know I am!' said Mrs Good-Manners in a fierce voice. 'I'm going to burst with rage!'

Tom slyly dug his pin into the back of Mrs Good-Manners' balloon-head.

BANG! It burst – and suddenly Mrs Good-Manners had no head at all. Amelia Jane gave a scream.

'Oh! She *has* burst! I've killed her

with my bad manners and rudeness!
Oh! Oh!'

The bear fell down on the ground
as soon as he heard the balloon burst
– so it looked as if Mrs Good-
Manners had tumbled flat. The toys,
trying to hide their giggles, all ran up.

'Oh, you wicked doll, Amelia!
You've made poor Mrs Good-
Manners burst with rage!'

'I didn't mean to, I didn't mean

to,' wept Amelia, who was now most alarmed.

'Poor, poor Mrs Good-Manners!' said the clockwork mouse. 'Now that's the end of her.'

'Oh, don't say things like that!' wept Amelia.

'You are a very bad doll to make people burst with rage at your rudeness,' said Tom sternly. 'Go and stand in the corner with your back to us for half an hour. We don't want to look at you.'

Amelia Jane was so frightened and sorry that she very humbly went into the corner and stood there, sniffing and crying. The toys quickly took the boots, shawl, and frock off the giggling teddy bear and threw them into the cupboard. They put the burst balloon-head into the wastepaper basket.

'Now we'll make a bargain with Amelia Jane,' whispered the bear. He cleared his throat, and spoke to Amelia.

'Amelia! Do you feel sorry for what you did? What are you going to do about it?'

'Oh, I do feel sorry, I do, I do,' sobbed Amelia. 'And I don't know *what* to do about it! Please, please don't tell anyone I've made Mrs Good-Manners burst with rage.'

'Well, suppose we keep the secret for you – are you going to behave better in future?' asked Tom sternly.

'Oh, much, much better,' said Amelia, wiping her eyes. 'I'll always say please and thank you and how-do-you-do – really I will!'

'Very well – you can come out of the corner and we'll give you another chance,' said Tom. 'We will never tell anyone what you've done.'

So Amelia came out of the corner and stared round to find Mrs Good-Manners. But she was gone, of course – and Amelia Jane never found out what had happened to her.

But – my goodness, what a difference there was in Amelia Jane's manners after that! You'd never have known she was the same doll. But how long it will last nobody knows.

Amelia Jane's Hair Goes Flat!

One day Amelia Jane quarrelled with the clockwork clown, who was playing with the picture-bricks very nicely and quietly all by himself in a corner. He was making a picture of some hens in a farmyard, and was turning each brick over and over to find bits of hens to fit into his picture.

Along came Amelia Jane and looked at the half-made picture. 'I'll help you,' she said.

'I don't want any help, thank you,' said the clockwork clown very politely. 'I like making pictures all by myself.'

'Don't be mean,' said Amelia, who did love poking her nose into what other people were doing. 'Let me help. Look – that brick shouldn't be there; I'm sure it shouldn't. It should be over here.'

She took hold of a brick that the clown had neatly fitted into place and put it somewhere else. It was quite wrong. The clockwork clown glared at Amelia.

'It should *not* be there,' he said, and put it back into its place.

'I tell you it should,' said Amelia, and she picked it up again. 'Look – that bit of hen's tail goes on to this bit of brown body.'

'Amelia Jane, you're wrong, and even if you were right I wouldn't want you to help,' said the clown crossly. 'I do like making pictures by myself. Go away.'

'Shan't!' said Amelia Jane.

'You jolly well will!' said the clown angrily. 'I'll push you to the other side of the nursery.'

'You couldn't. I'm too big,' said Amelia.

This was quite true. Amelia Jane was far too big to push. So the clockwork clown turned his back on her, said something rude under his breath, and went on with his brick picture by himself. Amelia Jane was angry.

'If you don't let me help, I'll throw all your bricks out of the window!' she said.

'You won't!' cried the clown, in horror.

'I just will!' shouted Amelia, quite losing her temper. And do you know, she picked up two bricks and threw them straight out of the window!

The clown was angry and dismayed. His lovely bricks! Now he couldn't make his picture. He was so cross that he picked up a brick and threw it straight at Amelia Jane.

Then, as you can imagine, Amelia went quite mad. She picked up all the bricks one by one and threw them right out of the window! Not one was left. The clown and the rest of the toys stared at Amelia in horror. What would the children say when they found all their lovely picture-bricks out on the grass?

'Look!' cried the clown suddenly. 'It's beginning to rain! Just look!'

So it was. The first big raindrops began to come down, splish-splash. Amelia Jane went rather red. She knew that rain spoilt things.

'It's going to pour, simply *pour*!' said the teddy bear. 'And I know what's going to happen to those bricks. The paper on them, that makes the pretty picture, is going to get soaking wet and peel off. Then there won't be any picture. That's what's going to happen.'

'Oh, Amelia Jane! It is *tire*some of you!' said Tom. 'Just because you lost your temper with the clown you spoil all the lovely bricks. You deserve to be punished.'

For once in a way Amelia Jane was ashamed of herself. She liked the picture-bricks, and had often made the hen-picture, the dog-picture, and the rabbit-picture. Now they would all be spoilt.

'I'll go out and bring in the bricks!' she cried suddenly. 'Yes, I will. I'm sorry I threw them out now, but I didn't know it was going to rain!'

'You'll get soaked!' cried the bear. But Amelia didn't listen. She ran to the door and down the passage to the stairs.

'Amelia! At least put something over your head!' cried the clown.

But Amelia wasn't going to stop for anything. She never did! Down the stairs she ran and into the garden. And my word, how the rain did pelt down! The raindrops hit Amelia Jane very hard, almost as if they were smacking her!

'Don't!' cried Amelia – but they

didn't stop, of course, and Amelia couldn't fight raindrops. She ran to the bricks and began to pick them up as fast as she could. They kept tumbling out of her arms, and she had to pick them all up again. The rain went on and on pouring down, and soaked Amelia Jane from head to foot. All the bounce came out of her hair and it hung down like rats' tails!

At last Amelia had all the bricks and she went indoors again. When she came into the nursery the toys cried out in horror: 'Amelia Jane! You are dripping wet!'

'Yes,' said poor Amelia, 'and I do feel cold and horrid. Here are the bricks. They are rather wet too. What are we going to do with them?'

'I'll put them into the hot-cupboard on the landing and let them dry slowly,' said Tom. 'Help me, Bear. And you had better take off your wet things, Amelia, and put on a nightie or something, so that your clothes can be dried in the hot-cupboard too.'

Whilst the toy soldier was taking the bricks to the hot-cupboard, Amelia Jane took off her wet things. She put on her nightie and a coat, and felt a bit warmer. The bear took her wet clothes to be dried in the hot-cupboard.

'What about your hair?' asked the clown, feeling it. 'Goodness! Isn't it wet! And all the bounce has come out, Amelia. It looks awfully flat and funny!'

'Perhaps the bounce will come back when it's dry,' said Amelia anxiously. 'Get a towel, Clown, and help me to dry it.'

So the clown, the toy soldier, the other dolls, the bear, and even the clockwork mouse all took a turn at rubbing Amelia's wet hair. Soon it was quite dry and Amelia brushed it out. But alas! It was now as straight and as flat as a poker, without a single wave anywhere! The rain had spoilt all the bounciness.

Amelia Jane cried. 'I have been asked to a party tomorrow. The children were taking me with them to Judy's birthday party. And I can't possibly go with hair like this. I look such a fright! Oh dear, I do wish I hadn't thrown those bricks out of the window like that! Then I wouldn't have needed to go out in the rain and get them.'

The toys really felt sorry for Amelia. She didn't look a bit like herself, sitting there with straight, flat hair and a very miserable face.

'Well, Amelia, you were very silly,' said the bear at last. 'But it's a pity if you have to have two punishments for

one silliness – having your hair all
straight and missing a party too! I
wonder if we could curl it for you.
How is hair curled, I wonder?'

'In curlers,' said Tom. 'A little girl
once came to stay the night here and
I saw her nanny putting her hair in
curlers.'

So the toys hunted for curlers but
they couldn't find any at all, which
was not surprising, for there were
none in the house. Then the clockwork
mouse had an idea.

'What about curl-papers?' he
squeaked. 'I know people sometimes
use bits of paper to twist hair up in,
and we could do that to Amelia Jane.'

So they hunted for an old
newspaper, or paper of any sort –

but there wasn't a piece to be found at all! Amelia Jane was quite in despair.

Then the clown looked into the toy-cupboard and saw the kite lying there, with its long tail made of twisted bits of paper.

'Look!' he cried. 'Just the very thing! Kite, may we borrow your tail, please? We will put all the papers back tomorrow.'

Well, the kite had seen how Amelia had run out into the rain to get the bricks, so he was quite willing for his tail to be used. The toys spent a long time untying the twists of paper that made his tail, but at last they had finished. And then they had some fun twisting Amelia Jane's long straight hair up in the bits of paper. Soon, she looked very funny indeed, with curl-papers all over her head!

'There! It won't be long before your hair is all nice and curly again!' cried the clown.

Amelia Jane kept the curl-papers in for a long time. In fact, she wouldn't take them out – and the children came into the nursery the next afternoon to look for her to take her to the party! *How* astonished they were to see Amelia Jane with curl-papers all over her head!

'Goodness, Amelia, who put those in?' they cried. 'What a funny sight you look!'

They took the curl-papers out – and you *should* have seen Amelia's hair! It was bouncier than it had ever been before, and when it was well-brushed it *did* look nice.

'You shall wear one of my very own hair-ribbons!' cried one of the children. So Amelia Jane went to the party very happily, wearing a bright red ribbon in her bouncy yellow hair.

'I'll bring you each back a sweet if I can,' she promised the toys. 'You've been really kind to me!'

And what about the curl-papers?

Well, the children threw them into the waste-paper basket because, you see, they didn't know that they had come off the tail of the kite! But the toys took them out of the basket, and, long before the children and Amelia Jane came back, they had tied the papers on to the tail of the kite again.

'I guess no other kite has a tail that was used for curl-papers!' cried the kite. And he was right!

Amelia Jane and the Snow-Doll

Did I ever tell you how Amelia Jane, that big naughty doll, made herself a snow-baby? She was really very funny about it.

One afternoon the snow fell thickly. Then it stopped, and the toys climbed up to the window-sill to look out.

'Isn't the snow pretty?' said the clockwork clown.

'Like a white blanket,' said the toy soldier. 'Let's go and play in it. The children are out, so we can slip into the garden and have some fun.'

'We'll make a snow-man!' said the teddy bear.

So out they all went. But Amelia Jane was very tiresome. She would keep snow-balling everybody, and as she was big and strong, her snowballs really hurt when they hit anyone. The clockwork mouse cried bitterly when one hit him on the nose.

'I'm sure it's bent my nose,' he sobbed. 'Is my nose bent, Tom?'

'Not a bit,' said Tom. 'And if it was it wouldn't matter. You would look just as sweet. Now, Amelia Jane, stop snowballing and come and help us to make a nice snow-man. It's really fun to do that, you know. We are going to give him an old hat belonging to the golden-haired doll, and there's an old scarf we can use, too. Come and help.'

But Amelia wouldn't. She stopped throwing snowballs, though. She watched the toys making the snow-man and then she thought of an idea herself.

'I'm going to make a snow-baby,' she said. 'A dear little snow-doll that I can dress up and keep for myself. Much better than a silly old snow-man.'

'Well, I do think you might come and help,' said the bear. 'It's much more fun when everyone gives a hand.

Don't be selfish, Amelia Jane.'

But Amelia Jane meant to have her own way. She gathered up handfuls of snow, and pressed them together. She made a neat little body and a dear little head. She put tiny stones into the head for eyes and a bit of stick for a mouth.

'Look at my baby snow-doll!' she cried. But the others wouldn't look.

They were cross with Amelia.

'Well, don't look then,' said Amelia. 'I shan't look at that silly snow-man of yours either. How stupid he is!'

'How do you know he is stupid if you haven't looked at him?' asked the bear cleverly. 'Ha, ha! You must have taken a peep then.'

'I'm going into the nursery to find a few clothes for my darling baby snow-doll,' said Amelia, in a huff. 'She shall be dressed properly – not wear just a hat and scarf like your silly snow-man.'

She went indoors. She found a dear little blue frock and a petticoat. She dragged a blue bonnet out of the doll's chest of drawers, and found a red coat. Now her snow-baby would look fine!

She went outside again and dressed the snow-doll. It wasn't at all easy, and Amelia Jane had to give up trying to get on the petticoat because it was too tight. But she managed to put on the dress and coat – and the little blue bonnet looked sweet!

'Look, Toys, look at my snow-doll!' cried Amelia Jane, proud of what she had done.

'You wouldn't look at our snow-man so we shan't look at your doll,' said the bear. 'That's quite fair, Amelia Jane.'

'Well, I still think your snow-man is silly and stupid, even without looking at him,' said Amelia. 'You can't even take him indoors with you. But I am going to take my dear little doll into the nursery with me, and keep her for a pet.'

The toys laughed. 'You are just as silly as you think our snow-man is!' said Tom.

Well, the toys went indoors, and had to leave their fine snow-man out in the garden, of course. He looked lovely with the old hat and scarf on. But Amelia Jane carried her baby snow-doll into the nursery, and looked at her lovingly. She was really very proud of her.

Amelia got into the toy-cupboard. She felt sleepy after her play in the snow.

'My snow-baby and I are going to have a little snooze,' she said to the toys. 'Please don't disturb us.'

'We wouldn't dream of it!' said Tom, with a grin.

Amelia Jane held her baby snow-doll tightly in her arms and shut her eyes. In half a second she was fast asleep.

'Look!' whispered the teddy bear.

'Amelia's snow-doll is melting because the nursery is warm. Had we better wake her up?'

'No. She said she didn't want to be disturbed,' said the clown. 'Leave her. See what she says when she wakes up! She will have a horrid shock!'

Well, Amelia Jane slept for an hour – and then she began having horrid dreams about falling into a river and getting cold and wet. She woke up with a jump – and oh, my goodness, whatever had happened? She was clasping a few wet clothes tightly to her – and she was soaked through and dripping wet! The snow-doll had disappeared.

'Oh!' cried Amelia, jumping up, startled. 'What has happened? I'm wet all over! Who has been watering me? Oh, you bad toys, standing laughing there – what have you done with my darling snow-baby? I am dripping wet. I shall get a cold. A-tish-oo!'

Well, nobody would tell Amelia what had happened, but all the toys laughed. Amelia had to go and dry herself by the fire, and she was very cross indeed.

Well, she thought, I do wonder what happened? Could my baby doll have melted and made me wet? Oh, I do hope that silly snow-man out in the garden has melted too!

She went to look. He was still there, as grand as could be and he laughed when he saw poor wet Amelia Jane!

'You've looked at me after all!' he seemed to say. 'Don't you think I look fine, Amelia Jane?'

But all Amelia said was, 'A-tish-oo!'

Amelia Jane is Naughty Again!

I'm going to tell you how naughty Amelia Jane, the big bad doll in the nursery, let the canary out of the cage.

There was a dear little canary in the nursery called Goldie. He hopped about from perch to perch and sang a merry carol of a song to the toys. They all loved him very much indeed, and when he dropped seeds out of his

341

cage on to the floor, they collected them in a little pot from the dolls' house and saved them in case they could ever give them back to him.

Now one day Amelia Jane thought she would like to look right into Goldie's cage and see the water-dish he had there, and the seed-dish, and the saucer he used for a bath.

So she got a chair and put it just under the cage. Then she climbed up the chair, and balanced herself very cleverly on the back. She caught hold of the side of the cage and pulled herself up to peep inside.

'Oh!' she said. 'Goldie has a dear little blue saucer for a bath. Goldie, do bath yourself so I can watch!'

So the canary bathed himself and sent silvery drops of water all over Amelia Jane. She laughed and wiped her face.

'Goldie, would you like to fly round the nursery?' said Amelia. 'You could stretch your wings nicely then.'

The toys listened in dismay. 'Amelia Jane! You know that Goldie is not allowed out of his cage unless there is somebody like Nanny or the children in the room to get him back!' cried the clown.

'Oh, I can get him back all right,' said Amelia, and she began to fumble with the catch of the cage-door.

'Amelia Jane! How dare you do such a thing!' shouted the teddy bear. 'Stop at once! You are not to let Goldie out.'

Well, of course, as soon as Amelia was told she mustn't do a thing she at once felt she must do it. So she slipped back the catch and opened the cage-door. And out hopped Goldie at once in great delight!

He spread his pretty yellow wings and flew all round the room, making quite a wind with them when he passed the watching toys!

'Oh, Goldie! Go back!' cried all the toys. But the little yellow canary didn't mean to! Not he! He had never been free before without the children or somebody in the room – and now he was really going to enjoy himself.

He flew to the top of the clock and sang a little song there. He flew to the mantelpiece and talked to the china duck that stood there. He had a really lovely time.

Tom shut the window. The bear pushed the door till it shut with a click. Then the toys looked at one another.

'*Now* what are we to do?' said the bear in despair.

'Tira-tirra-lee!' said the canary from the top of the toy-cupboard, and cocked his pretty little head on one side.

Amelia Jane looked inside the cage door. She wondered what it felt like to be inside such a nice little cage, with seed on one side, water on the other, the bath on the floor, and a little swing at the top.

'I'll squeeze myself in and see,' said Amelia with a chuckle. So she managed to squeeze herself in through the door, tearing her dress as she did so.

She almost got stuck, for she was a very big doll, but somehow or other she managed to get inside.

'Now I'm a canary!' she shouted to the astonished toys. 'I'm a canary and I'm going to sing!' And she opened her mouth as if it was a beak and tried to sing like Goldie. It was really very funny.

The clockwork clown had an idea.

Whilst Amelia Jane was singing he
hurriedly climbed up the chair and
stood on the back of it, almost falling
off. He just managed to reach the
door – and he shut it and latched it!

'Amelia Jane is caught!' he cried.
'She's shut in the cage!'

'It serves her right for letting
Goldie out!' said the bear. 'Hurrah!
Good for you, Clown! See how the
bad doll likes being shut up!'

Well, as soon as Amelia found that she was locked in, she didn't like it one bit. She turned to the door and jiggled it hard. But it wouldn't open.

'Let me out!' yelled Amelia, bumping her head against the swing at the top of the cage. 'Let me out! How horrid you all are!'

'You let Goldie out when you shouldn't, and now you've got a good punishment!' said the pink rabbit.

'You be quiet,' said Amelia rudely.

'Clown – Bear – Tom – please, please let me out!'

But the toys were now watching Goldie. They had heard the cat mewing outside the nursery door and they were afraid. Goldie would certainly be caught if the cat came in

– and how dreadful that would be!

'Goldie! Come into the dolls' house,' said the clown suddenly. 'We've got some of your seeds in there in a little dish, and you can eat them. We saved them for you when you scattered them on the floor from your cage.'

Goldie was feeling hungry, so he followed the clown to the pretty dolls' house in the corner. He thought it was a dear little house.

The clown opened the door and went in with the canary. As soon as the yellow bird was safely inside, Tom, who was outside, shut the door with a bang. Now the canary was safe!

The clown took the canary to the

kitchen and opened the little cupboard there. Inside was the little dish of seeds. As soon as the canary was eating them, sitting on a chair at the table, the clown slipped into the hall of the dolls' house, and went to the front door. In a moment he was outside and had shut the door! Good! Now the canary was quite safe and couldn't get out, because all the windows and doors were shut.

'Well, that's another good thing done!' said the clown, pleased. 'Amelia's caught – and the canary is safe!'

'Sh! Sh!' said the pink rabbit suddenly. 'Somebody is coming!'

'Gracious! And Amelia is in the cage!' said the little teddy bear.

They all scuttled to the toy-cupboard and lay down there, as still as could be. The door opened and in came Nanny. At first she didn't notice Amelia Jane in the cage and then she looked up and saw her. She stared and stared as if she couldn't really believe her eyes!

'Amelia Jane! In the canary's cage! And where is the canary?' cried the nanny in the greatest surprise. She hurried to the cage and looked inside.

'Why, the canary isn't here! Amelia Jane, what have you done with Goldie? Oh, you bad naughty doll, you are always in mischief of some sort!'

Nanny was very angry. She opened the cage-door and pulled

Amelia Jane out rather roughly. Then she sat her down hard in the corner. Amelia Jane was very miserable.

Nanny looked everywhere for the canary, but of course she couldn't see Goldie. And then the canary suddenly sang a little tune from the dolls' house, and peeped out of a window!

'Well, I never did!' cried Nanny, amazed. 'I must be dreaming! Amelia in the canary's cage – and the canary shut up in the dolls' house. Yes – I must be in bed and dreaming! But all the same I think I'll put Goldie back into his cage, dream or no dream!'

So she opened a window in the dolls' house, put in her hand and took hold of Goldie. She popped him back into his cage and shut the door. He was safe once more!

Then Nanny went out again to fetch the children from school. The toys peeped out from the cupboard at Amelia Jane. She was crying.

'How did you like being a canary in a cage?' asked the teddy bear.

'Sing us a little song!' said Tom.

'Spread your wings and fly!' said the pink rabbit.

And for once in a way Amelia didn't answer back. She just turned her back on the toys and sulked. But they didn't mind that, you may be sure!

Poor
Amelia Jane

Once it happened that some new
people came to live next door to the
house where Amelia Jane, the big
naughty doll, lived. This was most
exciting for the toys.

They did enjoy looking out of the
window and seeing all the new
furniture being taken out of the van.

'Oooh! What a big sideboard!'
said the teddy bear. 'How will it go in

at the front door?'

'Gracious! There must be lots of children there!' said Tom. 'I've seen three cots go in already.'

'One of them was a doll's cot, silly,' said Amelia Jane. 'I wonder if the new people will do anything to the garden. It's a dreadful mess.'

The new people did. They cut the grass and pulled up all the weeds. They pruned the trees and cut back the bushes. And then they dug a pond!

The toys were excited about that. '*We* haven't a pond in our garden,' said Amelia Jane. 'Now on moonlight nights we can take the toy boats and go and sail them there. And I can paddle.'

'That *will* be fun!' said the clockwork mouse. 'I must be careful not to drop my key in the pond, in case I can't find it again.'

The toys often sat on the window-sill watching the pond being dug. Then it was cemented all the way round, and crazy-paving was laid for an edging.

Then the pond was filled with water! It was great fun to watch. It trickled in and the pond was full by the evening.

And then the toys noticed something in the middle of the pond. It stuck out and seemed to be a kind of bowl with three little pipes.

'What's it for?' asked Amelia Jane.

'I think it is for a fountain,' said

the bear, who had overheard somebody saying this. He didn't know what a fountain was – but he felt rather grand saying it, all the same.

'What's a fountain?' said Amelia Jane. 'Is it anything like a mountain?'

The toys didn't know. They had never seen a mountain or a fountain either. They stared at the thing in the middle of the pond.

'Oh, well, never mind,' said Amelia. 'It's full moon tonight – what about taking the toy boats and going to sail them on the pond? That *would* be fun!'

So that night, when the moon was shining brightly, the toys all stole out of the nursery, and carried with them three little toy boats, a floating

duck, and the toy ship. This was
rather big, so the bear and Tom had
to carry it together. With giggles and
squeals they squeezed through the
hedge into the next-door garden.

The pond looked lovely, shining in
the moonlight. Amelia put one of the
toy boats on the water and it floated
beautifully. The pink rabbit put
another boat into the pond and
dragged it round and round by a bit
of string. The clockwork mouse had a

boat too. It was really fun.
Then the bear launched the
big ship, and it sailed right
across the pond itself,
bending sideways in the
breeze.

The floating duck was
overjoyed to have such a big piece of
water to swim on, because usually she
only had the bath. It was the
clockwork mouse who had thought of
bringing her, and she was really very
grateful to him.

'Clockwork Mouse, would you like
a sail on my back?' she called to him.

'Oh, I would,' said the mouse. 'All
the other toys can paddle, but I can't,
because I've only little wheels to run
on instead of legs. Do take me for a

ride on your back.'

'Clockwork Mouse, go to that funny thing in the middle of the pond and have a look at it!' said Amelia Jane suddenly. 'We can't wade there because the water gets too deep in the middle – but the duck can easily take you. Then you can climb up and run round the bowl there, and look into those three funny pipes.'

'He'd better not,' said the bear. 'We don't exactly know what that thing is for.'

'Oh, don't be so silly,' said Amelia, splashing the bear a little. She was paddling. 'What harm can he do?'

'Amelia Jane, if you splash me, I shall splash *you*!' said the bear crossly. Amelia Jane splashed him again.

Then the bear splashed Amelia so much that she ran out of the pond. 'You horrid bear! You've wetted my hair and you know it goes flat then. I don't like you!'

The clockwork mouse got on to the duck's back and the duck swam with him right to the middle of the pond. 'I think I'll just get off and look round this funny thing in the middle,' said the mouse. 'After all, I'm the only one that can really see what it is.'

So off he got and ran round the stone bowl. He looked into the three pipes too.

Now Amelia Jane was sulking a bit because the bear had driven her out of the pond by splashing so hard. She walked round to the other side of the pond – and she came across a pipe that led right down into the pond! And it had a tap on it. This was exciting!

Amelia Jane could never see a tap without turning it on, though she had been told again and again that it was a dangerous thing to do.

She tried to turn the tap – but it was very stiff. She used her right hand – then her left – and then she used both hands together!

The tap turned – and at the same moment the fountain began to play in the middle of the pond. *You* know what a fountain is, don't you? It's a big jet of water that gushes high into the air, turns over and falls back into the pond again! Well, that's just what happened when Amelia Jane turned on the tap!

Three jets of water gushed strongly out of the three pipes in the middle of the stone bowl in the pond, and sprang high into the air. They made a pretty arch before they fell back again, and all the toys stared in wonder at the fountain in the middle of the pond.

It shone in the moonlight. It made a pretty trickling noise – but what was that on top of it, jerking up and down on the water?

It was the poor little clockwork mouse! He had been looking at the pipes at exactly the same moment as Amelia had turned on the fountain – and the jets of water sprang high into the air and took him with them!

The mouse was astonished and frightened. He was jerked up and down at the top of the fountain, and he just couldn't do anything about it! The water held him there, and he couldn't get down.

He began to squeak and squeal, and the toys stared in fright.

'The clockwork mouse is on top of the fountain! Look! He can't get out of it! It's bouncing the poor little thing up and down, up and down, and he must be getting terribly wet!'

Nobody knew that the fountain had been made because Amelia turned the tap on. But Amelia knew it, of course, and she tried her hardest to turn off the tap again. But she couldn't. Then she called to the toys to come and help but nobody was strong enough, not even Tom.

'Oh, you *are* tiresome, Amelia Jane!' said the pink rabbit, almost in tears, for he was very fond of the little mouse. 'You told the mouse to go and look at the fountain-thing – and then you go and turn on this tap and make the fountain come, and take the mouse up into the air with it! Now what are we going to do? The mouse will go on being bounced at the top of the fountain all night long!'

Amelia Jane was worried too. She didn't like to think of that. Whatever could be done? She tried to turn the tap off again – but it was far too stiff!

'I'd rescue him myself, but I can't

walk,' said the toy duck. 'I'm no good out of the water.'

'Amelia Jane – you got the mouse into trouble, so you should be the one to get him out again,' said the bear, looking at the big doll.

'I know,' said Amelia. 'Well – there's only one way to rescue him, and that is for me to wade out into the very deep part, climb into the bowl, and try to reach the mouse with my hands. But the fountain will play over me if I do.'

'Serves you right,' said Tom.

Amelia Jane pulled her skirts above her knees and waded into the cold water. She took a few steps towards the middle of the pond. 'Ooooh! It's getting deep!' she said.

So it was – very deep! It was
right above her waist by the time she
got to the fountain. She pulled herself
up into the stone bowl, which was
now, of course, full of water. And then

the fountain played all over poor Amelia Jane!

It wetted her yellow hair and her face. It wetted her shoulders and ran down her neck! And when she reached up her arms to try to grab the clockwork mouse from the top of the fountain, the water ran down her sleeves! It went into her eyes and mouth, too, and she choked and spluttered.

But she got the mouse! She took hold of him and put him on her shoulder. Then she climbed down from the stone bowl into the pond again, and waded back to the bank. The clockwork mouse jumped down to the ground and shook himself free from the thousands of water drops all over him!

'Oh, that *was* a horrid adventure!' he squealed. The toys looked at him and hoped he wouldn't have a cold. If he had a cold and sneezed, his key flew out at each sneeze, and that was such a nuisance.

The toys all went back to the nursery, and Amelia Jane dripped like a fountain all the way! She had to undress herself, and sit in dry underwear in front of the gas-fire for the rest of the night. Her hair went all flat, and she really looked dreadful.

'Well, it's a good punishment for you for interfering,' said Tom. 'But as you rescued the mouse so bravely, I really can't help feeling sorry for you. I'll put your hair in curl-papers if you like, and I'll help the bear to iron your clothes with the iron out of the dolls' house, when they are dry.'

'Thank you, Tom,' said Amelia, in a very small voice.

'Could you iron my tail too?' asked the mouse. But Tom said no, tails weren't meant to be ironed *or* put into curl-papers either.

When morning came, Amelia Jane was dry, her clothes were ironed, and her hair all bouncy again – and the clockwork mouse didn't get a cold, so things weren't as bad as they might have been!

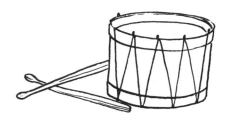

Amelia Jane and the Drum

All the toys were as quiet as could be because Nanny was in the room ironing. None of them ever moved or spoke when anyone was in the room.

'Bump-bump,' went Nanny's iron over the ironing-board. 'Bump-bump.'

Tom and the baby doll were feeling proud because Nanny had washed their clothes that morning, and was now ironing them. How clean and pretty they would look in their freshly washed clothes!

Nanny finished ironing the little jackets, trousers, petticoats and dress.

She went to the nursery fireplace, and hung the little clothes on the brass rail round the guard to air.

Then she went out of the room to dress the children up nicely for their afternoon walk. Tom spoke up as soon as she had gone.

'Doesn't my jacket look lovely! Just look at it hanging there, so bright and clean!'

'And look at my lacy petticoats!' said the golden-haired doll, pleased. 'They will feel so nice and clean when I put them on again.'

Amelia Jane walked out of the toy-cupboard, and the toys followed her. 'What shall we play at?' asked Amelia. 'Let's play ring-a-ring-of-roses.'

'No, it's really too hot,' said the clockwork clown. 'Nanny has got the fire on today, and the sun is pouring in through the window. It's too hot to do anything but sit about and talk.'

'I *want* to play!' said Amelia Jane. So of course she made them all play with her! She was such a big doll and so strong that usually the toys just had to do what she told them. So there they were, tearing round and round in a big ring on the floor, singing ring-a-ring-of-roses in their small high voices.

'All fall down!' they cried. And

down they all fell. The clockwork clown wouldn't get up again.

'No, really it's too hot,' he said. 'You look very hot yourself, Amelia Jane. You look red and ugly. Let's sit quietly and talk.'

'Dear me, if you're as hot as all that I'll open the window for you!' said Amelia Jane, who was feeling the heat herself by now.

'No, don't do that,' said the teddy  bear. 'Nanny said she didn't want the window open because the wind was so strong.'

'I shall do as I like!'

said Amelia Jane. And, as usual, she did! She went to the window-seat, climbed up on it, and got on to the window-sill. She undid the catch of the window and swung it wide open.

In came the wind at once. Whoo-oooo-ooooo-oooh!

'Oh, Amelia Jane! How naughty you are!' cried the clockwork clown. 'The wind has blown over the vase of flowers on the table. Look what a mess the water is making.'

'Nanny can clear it up,' said Amelia.

'And, oh, look, look, look!' suddenly squealed the golden-haired doll. 'The wind is blowing our clean clothes off the guard into the fender. They'll go into the fire. Oh, oh, what shall we do? Shut the window, Amelia Jane!'

But Amelia Jane couldn't! It had stuck and she wasn't strong enough to pull it back again. She stared at the little clothes blowing off the guard. The prettiest lace petticoat blew right into the fire and was burnt up!

'Oh!' screamed the golden-haired doll. 'There goes my best petticoat! Oh, you bad, mischievous doll!'

Amelia Jane didn't know what to do. She certainly was a bad doll, but all the same she didn't want to see the clothes burnt in the fire. The toys would never forgive her.

She called loudly: 'Nanny. Nanny! Come quickly!'

But Nanny didn't come. So Amelia

called again: 'Nanny! Nanny!'

Still Nanny didn't come. She
didn't hear. 'Oh, what shall I do?'
cried Amelia Jane. The golden-haired
doll sobbed. Tom glared at Amelia.

Then Amelia had a bright idea.
She rushed to the toy-cupboard. She
reached right to the back of it, and
took out the toy drum. She found
two sticks. And then
she went to the
nursery door and
banged hard on that
little drum.

'Rum-ti-tum-
ti-tum! Rum-ti-
tum-ti-tum!
Rr-rr-rr-rr-rr-rr-rr!
Rum-ti-tum-ti-tum!'

You should have heard the noise! My goodness, it was deafening! Nanny heard it. The children heard it. They listened in great astonishment.

'That's my drum!' cried the little boy. 'Who is playing it? Who can it be?'

The two children and Nanny ran to see. As soon as Amelia heard them coming she flung the drum down on the floor and raced back to the toy-cupboard with the toys. They sat down there and kept as still as could be. Nanny and the children could see nothing at all when they came into the nursery – except the little drum thrown down on the floor with its two sticks lying beside it.

'How funny!' said Nanny. 'Who

played the drum? And why?'

'Nanny! Nanny! The dolls' clothes are blowing off the guard into the fire!' cried the little girl. 'Oh look!'

Nanny rushed to save them. Alas, they were all dirty again now, and would have to be washed and ironed once more. And one petticoat was quite gone.

'Who opened that window?' said Nanny crossly. 'I left it shut. I knew the clothes would blow into the fire if the wind came into the room. And look – it's blown over the flowers on the table, too. What a mess! I wish I knew who had opened that window. They deserve a good telling off.'

Amelia Jane went red. The toys looked at her and nodded their heads.

Yes – she did deserve a good telling off!

When Nanny and the children had gone out for their walk the baby doll spoke angrily to naughty Amelia Jane.

'I shan't be able to wear my

clothes today. All because of you, Amelia Jane. Nanny is right – you do deserve a good scolding.'

'And what about my clothes, too?' said Tom gloomily. 'My trousers were scorched by the flames. They will never look so nice again, just round the waist.'

Amelia Jane was very red. She took off her new hair-ribbon and held it out to Tom. 'You can have this to tie round your waist for a sash,' she said. 'Then it will hide the bit that is scorched. And Golden-haired Doll – I will get six of my little handkerchiefs and sew them together to make a small petticoat for you.'

'Well, it is nice of you to try and make up for what we have lost,' said the golden-haired doll. 'Perhaps we won't be cross with you after all.'

'Well, I *did* think of the drum and beat it to get somebody here to rescue your clothes,' said Amelia Jane. 'Didn't I?'

'Yes, that was clever of you,' said Tom. 'All right we'll forgive you this once, Amelia. But DON'T BE SILLY AGAIN!'

BOOK THREE

Amelia Jane is Naughty Again!

Contents

Amelia Jane's Necklace

You remember Amelia Jane, don't you, the naughty doll who lives in the nursery with Tom the toy soldier and the teddy bear and all the other toys?

She's still there – and still naughty, though she does sometimes turn over a new leaf. But, as Tom says, it's never a very *big* leaf, and doesn't seem to last long.

Now, one day Tom went exploring in the toy-cupboard, and he found an old cardboard box. It rattled when he shook it, and he wondered what could be inside.

'Open it and see,' said the teddy bear. So Tom opened it. He and the bear stared at what was inside. They

didn't at all know what the little brown things there were.

'Are they nice big beads?' said Tom.

'They might be something to eat,' said the bear, but he couldn't even nibble a hole in one of the smooth brown things.

The sailor doll strolled up to look. 'Oh, they are *acorns*,' he said. 'Didn't you know *that*?'

'What are acorns?' asked Tom, who had never heard of them in his life.

The sailor doll didn't know, but he pretended to. 'Oh, they are things that can be used for a bead necklace,' he said, remembering that he had once seen the children stringing them together. 'Yes, acorn beads, I suppose. They would make quite a nice necklace, wouldn't they?'

'Oh,' said the bear suddenly. 'Tom, do you think *I* might have an acorn necklace to wear round my neck? Ever since I lost my blue bow I've felt very cold about my neck. I should so like a necklace. It would keep my neck very warm.'

'Well, Teddy, we'll thread you one,' said Tom, who was always very kind. 'Now let me see – what do we want for threading beads?'

'A sharp needle – and some string,' said the sailor doll. 'Look – somebody has already made holes through the acorns, ready for threading. They must have done that and then forgotten all about them.'

Amelia Jane came up, full of curiosity. 'What's that you've got?' she said.

'Acorns,' said Tom, and turned away. He wasn't pleased with Amelia Jane. She had knocked his hat off that morning and pulled out a tuft of his hair to make whiskers for another toy.

'Acorns! What are they?' said Amelia.

'BEADS!' said the sailor doll. 'But NOT for you. For the teddy bear, because he's lost his blue bow.'

'Well, I've lost the lace out of my shoes,' said Amelia Jane. 'I don't see why I shouldn't have the beads as much as the bear.'

'What's losing a shoe-lace got to do with having a necklace?' asked Tom.

'Quite a lot,' said Amelia, who could always argue for hours. 'You see, if I can't have a shoe-lace, I might as well have a neck-lace.'

'Don't be silly,' said the bear. 'You always want everything. Well, you're not going to have *this*!'

The sailor doll, the bear and the toy soldier took the box of acorn beads away to a corner. Amelia Jane

followed them.
They wondered
where to get a
needle and
thread.

'There are
some in the work-
basket,' said Amelia Jane.
Tom climbed up to the
table to get a needle and
some strong thread. He
found a little roll of
string there and
decided that would
do nicely.

Down he came. But, of course,
nobody could thread the little needle

with the thick string.

'Oooh!' said Tom. 'That's the second time I've pricked myself.'

'Bother this,' said the bear, trying hard to push the end of the string through the needle eye. 'It won't go. Oh dear – now *I've* pricked myself!'

'Let *me* try,' said Amelia Jane, and she took up the string. She saw at once that it wouldn't go through the eye of the little needle. She looked at the holes in the acorns. They were big – quite big enough to take the string without a needle to drag it through.

'*I'll* show you!' said Amelia, and she picked up an acorn in her left hand. She ran the string through the hole in it and then picked up another.

'See? Quite easy! You are always so stupid. I'll thread the whole lot now.'

She threaded all the acorns very quickly. She really was clever at things like that.

'Thanks,' said Tom, when she had threaded the whole lot. 'That's fine. Now I'll put the necklace round the bear's neck. It will suit him.'

But Amelia Jane put it round her own! And what is more, she tied the string very tightly into a firm knot. She grinned round at the toys. 'It's mine!' she said, touching the necklace. 'I threaded it, didn't I?'

Well, what was to be done about *that*? Tom was so cross that he held Amelia Jane's arms, whilst the sailor doll tried to undo the knot of the necklace. But he couldn't possibly, because it was much too tight. So they had to give it up and marched off to the toy-cupboard very crossly indeed.

'Mean thing! She's always doing things like that,' said the bear. 'And I did so want a necklace for my throat, now I've lost my blue bow. I do feel upset.'

'It's just like Amelia Jane,' said the sailor doll, gloomily. 'Why didn't we think of her putting it on as soon as she'd finished it? Now we shall never have it, and she'll keep on and on saying, "Look at my beautiful new necklace!"'

That is just what Amelia Jane did say, of course! Whenever anyone came to visit the toys, she would show them her necklace. 'Isn't it lovely?' she would say. 'It's made of acorns. I've heard that they are very, very precious. I made this necklace all by myself!'

Now, that summer was very, very hot. The nursery children went away to the sea, and the toys were left by themselves in the nursery.

'I can't stand this heat,' said

Amelia Jane, one day. 'I'm going out into the garden – and I'm going to undress and get into the pond to cool myself. It's no use saying I mustn't, because I'm GOING to!'

Well, she did, of course. She took off all her clothes except her underwear, which was sewn on and wouldn't come off, and she got into the water at the edge of the garden pond. She lay right down in it, with her head against the edge of the pond, and kicked and splashed in joy.

'It's lovely! It's so cold!' she called. 'Come along and enjoy yourselves, toys! Ooooh! This is delicious!'

The other toys paddled. They were

afraid of undressing and getting right
into the water in case somebody came
in quickly and didn't give them time
to dress and get back to the toy-
cupboard. But Amelia Jane never
cared about things like that.

She spent all day in the water, and
the next day, too, lying there in her
underwear and acorn necklace,

enjoying herself thoroughly. She frightened the sparrows who came to bathe, and she splashed the freckled thrush when he flew down. She really was full of mischief those hot, summer days, and soon no toy liked to go near the pond for fear of being soaked to the skin by Amelia Jane.

Now, if acorns are soaked in water for hours and hours they begin to grow! An acorn is the seed of an oak tree, and if it is made damp, it wants to put out a root and a shoot, like all seeds.

And Amelia Jane's acorns were no different from any other acorns. When they felt the water round them, soaking into them, they rejoiced, and grew fat. They wanted to burst their skins, and put out little white roots and shoots, to grow into tiny oak-trees!

Nobody noticed that the acorns had grown fat. Amelia Jane didn't, of course, because nobody can see what is tightly threaded round their neck. But when the acorns burst their skins a little, and put out white roots, Tom saw them, and gave a scream.

'What's the matter?' said the bear.

Tom pointed to Amelia Jane's neck. 'Look! Her necklace is growing white worms! Ugh, how horrible. Worms down her neck!'

Everyone stared at Amelia Jane's

neck. She didn't like it at all. 'What's the matter?' she said. 'What's all this about worms?'

'Oh, Amelia Jane – it's quite true. Your necklace has got white worms in it,' said the sailor doll. 'They are wriggling out of the acorns. That's where they live, I suppose! Oooh, how horrible!'

'I don't believe you,' said Amelia, and she put up her hand to her necklace. She touched one or two of the growing white roots and gave a scream. 'Oh, I touched a worm! I did, I did! Oh, whatever shall I do?'

'Well, you *would* take the necklace,' said the bear, quite pleased. 'It's your own fault. You shouldn't have been so selfish.'

Amelia Jane stood trembling in the nursery. 'Will they crawl down my neck?' she said, looking pale.

'I expect so,' said the bear, who was quite enjoying himself. 'If I were a worm I'd crawl all over you.'

Amelia screamed again. 'Don't! I can't bear it. Take them away! Undo

my necklace, quick!'

'Certainly not,' said the sailor doll.

'You wanted to wear it, and you
jolly well can!'

'I'll undo it myself,' said Amelia,
but she couldn't. That knot was tied so
tightly that she couldn't possibly undo
it herself. And nobody else would.

'You can go on wearing worms,'
said the bear. 'Fancy wearing a worm
necklace! Ha, ha! It suits you, Amelia.'

'Please, please do untie the knot,'
begged the big doll. 'Where are the
scissors? We can cut the string.'

But there were no scissors to be
found. The work-basket had gone, and
not one of the toys had any scissors of

their own. So Amelia had to go on wearing her peculiar necklace.

She was very, very miserable. The toys watched the 'worms' growing longer each day, as the roots pushed out from the acorns. 'They're getting bigger, Amelia,' said the bear. 'And longer. And fatter. Ooooooh! I wonder if those worms will get hungry, Amelia Jane, and nibble you.'

Amelia sobbed with fright. What could she do? The toy soldier was sorry for her and tried to undo the knot, but he couldn't. 'Go out into the garden and see if the worms will drop down and join the brown worms in the grass,' he said.

So Amelia went out and stood in the garden. And whilst she was there the string, which had got rather wet and rotten at the front of her neck, suddenly broke. And down fell all the acorns, with their funny white roots and tiny shoots.

'They've gone!' yelled Amelia, and fled indoors. The toys went out to see. There lay the acorns, with the white 'worms' sticking out of them.

'Let's bury them in the ground, then perhaps these white worms will go and join their brother brown worms,' said the sailor doll.

So they dug little holes and put the split acorns, with their roots and shoots, carefully in the earth.

And, would you believe it, they all grew into tiny little oak-trees, with strong, white roots delving deep into the ground, and little shoots that bore leaves in the sunshine!

But Amelia Jane didn't know that. She never went near that part of the garden, in case those white worms saw her and went after her.

Poor Amelia! She says she is never going to wear a necklace again, and I don't expect she ever will. The bear says it serves her right – but it really was very funny, wasn't it?

Amelia Jane and the Ink

Amelia Jane was in a very bad mood, and when Tom the toy soldier asked her to play with him, she pushed him away and started to quarrel with him.

'You can't play games,' Amelia Jane shouted. 'You are so stupid.'

'I'm not stupid,' said Tom.

'Yes, you are,' said Amelia Jane.

'Stop it, you two,' said the bear.
'Don't take any notice of Amelia
Jane, Tom.'

'It's difficult not to,' said Tom.

The toys began to talk together,
but they wouldn't talk to Amelia.
When she was in one of her silly
moods, they just took no notice of her.

She didn't like that. 'Be quiet, stop talking,' she said. 'I'm going to write a letter.'

'Well, write it. We don't care!' said the bear. 'Who are you going to write it to?'

'Father Christmas,' said Amelia.

'Well, tell him to come and take you away and put you in his sack, and pop you into a stocking in some other nursery,' said Tom.

Amelia Jane was angry. 'You're unkind,' she said. 'I shall write to him – but I shall ask him to come and take *you* away. So there. You'll be sorry you were nasty to me, then.'

Tom felt rather frightened. He

wasn't at all sure that Father Christmas might not do what Amelia said.

'Father Christmas never reads any letters unless they are written in ink,' he said at last. He knew Amelia Jane only had a pencil to write with.

She looked at him. He said it so loudly that she thought it must be true. 'All right!' she said. 'I'll write my letter in ink then!'

The toys stared at her in horror. Not even the children in the nursery were allowed to write in ink. Their mother said they were not old enough. So the ink was always kept out of reach on the mantelpiece.

'Amelia Jane! You'd never dare to write in *ink*!' said the bear.

'Wouldn't I?' said Amelia. 'Well, you just see! I shall write my letter in ink, with a pen, and I shall blot it properly and everything.'

'You can't reach the ink,' said the bear.

'I can,' said Amelia.

'You're not to,' said the clockwork clown.

'I just shall then,' said Amelia. She went to the coal-scuttle and climbed up on top of it. From there she climbed on to the top of the nursery fireguard, which went all round the hearth.

Then she leaned on the mantelpiece

to try and reach the bottle of ink. She
just could!

She edged it carefully towards her.
Then she took the bottle into her hands.
'I've got it!' she cried. 'Look!'
She turned to show the toys –
and lost her balance! She fell off the

guard on to the hearth-rug – bump!
The bottle of ink flew into the air and
then fell bang on to Amelia's head. Its
cork shot out and the ink poured all
over Amelia's face! Some went into
her mouth. She spat it out at once.

'Poof! It's horrid!'

The toys stared at Amelia Jane in horror. Her face was blue all over. She did look funny. The toys didn't like her at all. She didn't look like Amelia Jane. She looked rather fierce and wild.

'What's the matter?' said Amelia

Jane, as the toys began to edge away from her.

'We don't like you. You're all blue in the face now,' said the bear.

'As blue as the sailor doll's trousers,' said Tom.

'You frighten me!' squealed the clockwork mouse, and raced into the toy-cupboard as if a cat were after him.

'Don't be silly,' said Amelia, trying to wipe her face with her hand. It made her hand blue. She stared at it and wondered what she looked like. There was a mirror over the book-case. Amelia Jane pushed a chair by the book-case, climbed up it and stood on the top of the book-case. She looked at herself in the mirror there.

'Oh! Oh!' she squealed. 'It isn't me! It isn't me! I'm somebody else! Oh, where have I gone? It isn't me!'

The toys looked at her. Certainly Amelia Jane didn't look like herself at all.

'There's only one thing to do, Amelia,' said Tom. 'You'll have to scrub your face!'

'Yes, I will, I will,' sobbed poor Amelia, taking another look at herself in the mirror, and then scrambling quickly down to the floor. 'Tom, get a scrubbing-brush, quick.'

Tom went to the basin and

climbed up on to the chair below. He knew there was a nail-brush there. He took it and rubbed it on the soap. Then he climbed down and went to Amelia Jane.

'Shall I do the scrubbing?' he asked. Amelia nodded. So Tom began to scrub her face. How he scrubbed!

'The soap's gone in my eye!' yelled Amelia Jane. Tom took no notice.

'Now it's in the other eye!' sobbed Amelia. 'Don't scrub so hard.'

Tom went on scrubbing. 'You're scrubbing my face away,' wailed poor Amelia. 'Don't scrub my nose so hard. Oh, it'll come off, I know it will!'

All the toys stood round, grinning. They couldn't help thinking that it was a very good punishment for Amelia Jane, after quarrelling with Tom so much, and trying to take the ink.

How he scrubbed! Amelia sobbed and cried, and her eyes smarted with the soap, but Tom wouldn't stop until her face was perfectly clean again. All the toys cheered him on. At last his arm ached and he put down the nail-brush.

'There,' he said, 'now you're all right.'

'Thank you,' sobbed Amelia. 'Oh dear, oh dear, why ever did I say I'd write in ink? Look at the mess on the hearthrug!'

Poor Amelia had to set to work and scrub that clean too. She put the empty bottle of ink back on the mantelpiece, feeling very guilty.

'You ought to look in your money-box and put some money by the bottle to pay for some more ink,' said the bear.

So Amelia looked in her money-box and put five coins on the mantelpiece by the bottle. The children found them there the next day, and they *were* surprised!

'Where did this money come from?' they wondered, and they turned to look at the toys. 'Goodness – isn't Amelia's face clean! Whatever has happened to it?'

They might have guessed when they found that their nail-brush was blue with ink – but they didn't!

As for Amelia Jane, she told Tom she was sorry she had quarrelled with him – so one good thing came out of her naughty prank, after all!

Amelia Jane's Boomerang

Amelia Jane found a toy boomerang at the back of the cupboard. Do you know what a boomerang is? It is a bit of curved wood made in such a way that it will always come back to the one who throws it.

You can see the boomerang Amelia Jane found if you look at the picture. She didn't know what it was, at first. Then, when she threw it into the air and found that it came back to her, she was thrilled.

'Now I'll have some fun!' she cried, and she threw the boomerang at the chimneys on the dolls' house! It knocked them off and they slid down the roof, fell to the ground and gave the clockwork mouse a terrible fright.

The boomerang flew back to Amelia Jane, and she caught it. 'Now I'll take off the sailor doll's hat!' she said with a giggle, and threw it again. It neatly took off the sailor doll's hat, and came back to Amelia Jane. She laughed at the sailor doll's look of

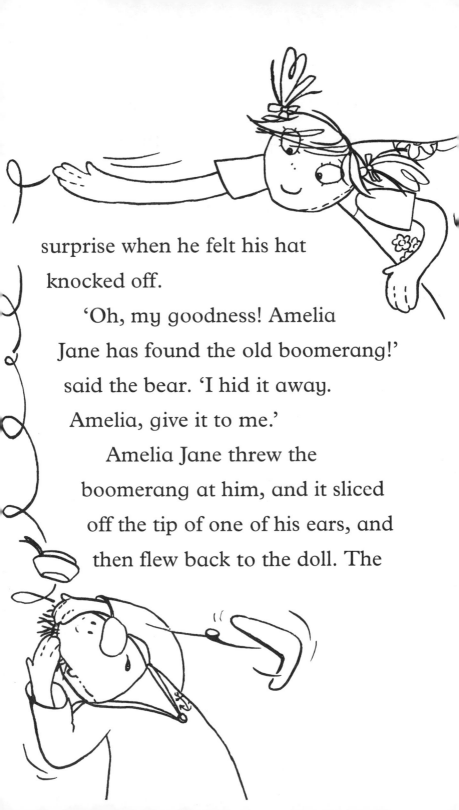

surprise when he felt his hat
knocked off.

'Oh, my goodness! Amelia
Jane has found the old boomerang!'
said the bear. 'I hid it away.
Amelia, give it to me.'

Amelia Jane threw the
boomerang at him, and it sliced
off the tip of one of his ears, and
then flew back to the doll. The

bear was very angry.

He ran at Amelia to get the boomerang. But she flung it at him again and he fell over. The boomerang returned to her hand. She laughed excitedly.

'It's no good! I'm *awfully* good with this. If you come rushing at me I'll throw it at you. So keep away. Now watch – I'm going to throw it at the snapdragons in that vase! I'll chop off some of their heads!'

And that's just what she did! The boomerang flew through the air, hit two snapdragons, broke their pretty heads, and then came flying back to the naughty doll.

Amelia Jane had a lovely time that day. She knocked the little china dog off the mantelpiece with her boomerang and he fell on to the hearth and broke a bit off one paw. She threw it at the little mouse who came for crumbs, and he lost two of his whiskers. And she threw it at the railway train and cut the funnel right off.

'How can we stop it?' said the clockwork clown in despair. He had had his hat knocked off six times by the boomerang and now he had stuffed it into his pocket for safety.

'I know where the old pop-gun is,' said the pink cat suddenly. 'Shall we

get that? It's got a cork on a string, and it always jerks back when it's shot out. You put the cork into the end of the gun, press the trigger – and out shoots the cork. But because it's on a string it always jerks back to the shooter again, like the boomerang goes back to Amelia Jane.'

This was quite a long speech for the pink cat to make, and everyone listened to it, except Amelia Jane, who was trying to knock down a silver thimble left on the mantelpiece.

'Yes! Get the pop-gun!' cried the bear, so the pink cat went to get it. He brought it out of an old box and showed it to the others. Tom the toy soldier fitted the cork into the end. It was on a long string tied to the gun. He pressed the trigger.

POP! Out flew the cork quite fiercely, and hit the bear on the right paw. He gave a yell. 'Don't practise on me, silly! That stung! Practise on Amelia Jane!'

Tom grinned. He went over to Amelia Jane and pointed the pop-gun at the back of her head.

POP! The cork flew out, caught her hair-ribbon, and then jerked back on its string.

Amelia Jane got a terrible shock.

'Oh! What was that?' she cried, and swung round at once.

'We've got a boomerang-cork!' grinned Tom, and shot at her again. POP! The cork hit her on the nose, and she almost fell over.

'Now you stop that!' cried Amelia Jane, 'or I'll throw my boomerang at you!'

'Well, every time you throw your boomerang we're going to shoot you with the pop-gun!' said Tom, putting the cork into the gun again. 'There's no reason why we shouldn't have a bit of fun, too! Look out!'

Pop! The cork hit Amelia Jane right in her middle and she gave a squeal.

'Oh! Oh! You've hit my dinner! Wait
till I get that horrid cork! I'll throw it
away!'

But she couldn't get the cork
because it was tied
on with
string to
the gun,
and it
always jerked back
when it was fired out.

The toys had a
wonderful time
chasing her round the nursery,
popping the cork at her. She didn't
have a chance to throw the
boomerang at them.

433

'You're very unkind,' she sobbed as she tried to dodge the toys.

'Oh, no – we're only doing the sort of thing you've been doing,' said Tom. 'You give us your boomerang and we'll give you the pop-gun. Then we can each have a turn at throwing the boomerang too.'

'No,' said Amelia. 'You'd only throw that at me as well. Promise not to and I'll give it to you.'

They promised, and Amelia Jane handed over the boomerang. Tom at once went to hide it away where it would never be found again. But, oh dear, Amelia Jane didn't promise not to shoot at the toys with the pop-gun, and the very first thing she did was to point it at the bear and fire.

POP! It flew out and hit him so hard in his tummy that it made him growl. But she couldn't shoot the cork again because Tom had cut the string and it didn't jerk back to the gun!

'Aha!' said the sailor doll, picking up the loose cork and putting it into his pocket, 'you won't do *that* again, naughty Amelia Jane!

Go and stand in the corner till we say you can come out. If you don't, we'll take the gun, tie on the string to the cork and do a bit of shooting again!'

So Amelia Jane is standing in the corner, sulking, and I rather think the toys are going to forget about her for a very long time!

Amelia Jane and the Scribbles

One day Amelia Jane found a red pencil on the floor. Somebody had dropped it there and forgotten to pick it up. Amelia Jane was pleased.

'Now I can write things in red,' she said. 'Look, this is a pencil that writes in red, Toys.'

'Well, if you think you're going to

write in my notebook, you're wrong,' said Tom.

'And if you think I'm going to lend you my little drawing-book to scribble in, you can think again,' said the teddy bear.

'And don't you dare to scribble inside the lid of the brick-box,' said the clockwork clown. 'I spent ages rubbing out some silly scribbles the pink cat did once with a bit of coal.'

'I don't know why you're so sharp with me,' said Amelia Jane. 'Anyone would think I wanted to do something naughty.'

'It's not at all surprising that we should think that,' said the bear.

'You've been fairly good for about a week. That's about as long as you *can* be good for.'

Amelia Jane badly wanted to scribble with her red pencil, but nobody would lend her any paper at all. So she got cross and went inside the toy-cupboard all by herself. When she came out,

she was smiling.

'Now, what's she smiling like that for?' said Tom, and he went inside the toy-cupboard. He gave an angry cry, and the toys went to see why.

'Look!' he said, pointing to the wall at the back of the cupboard. 'Look what she's done.'

The toys looked. Written across the wall were lots of words: '*The toy soldier is silly. The teddy bear is too fat. The clockwork clown is clumsy. The clockwork mouse is a baby.*'

'Look at that!' said the clown. 'How disgraceful! Doesn't Amelia Jane know that no decent people ever scribble on walls? Only the very lowest toys do that!'

They went to find Amelia, but they couldn't. But they found something scribbled on the wall near the toy-cupboard, at the bottom:

'*You're all sillies! I shall do what I like, so there! Signed, Amelia Jane.*'

'Isn't she awful?' said the bear. 'Now we shall have to spend ages rubbing this out before anyone sees it. Go and borrow some dusters from the dolls in the dolls' house, Tom.'

But when he got to the dolls' house, he found all the small dolls in a very bad temper.

'Somebody's been in and scribbled over our walls,' said Dinah, the mother doll. 'Look. Someone's written: "*This is a silly dolls' house.*"'

'What a shame,' said the bear. 'That's Amelia Jane. She wants scribbling on herself!'

'That's an awfully good idea of yours, bear,' said the clown. 'If only we could! That would soon stop her silly tricks!'

'Listen,' said the bear, thinking out a plan. 'We're giving a party tomorrow night, aren't we, to all the pixies who live in the garden outside? Well, let's wait till Amelia Jane is asleep tonight, and we'll scribble something across her forehead! She won't know, because she hardly ever looks at herself in the mirror, even to do her hair.'

All the toys giggled. That would be a good joke! They spent quite a lot of time rubbing out the things Amelia Jane had scribbled everywhere, and the big doll peeped out from behind the curtain, and laughed. She didn't know what they were planning for her, or she would have been on her guard.

That night Amelia Jane climbed up into one of the dolls' cots and lay down to sleep. She felt tired. She had done such a lot of writing that day! The toys waited till she was fast asleep, and then Tom climbed up softly to the cot. He sat down gently beside Amelia Jane.

'Pass me the paint-box,' he whispered, and the bear passed it up. A bright red colour was already mixed for him, and the paint-brush was there as well.

Tom began to paint words quickly on Amelia Jane's big smooth forehead. '*This is naughty Amelia Jane*' he put, and tried not to giggle.

Amelia Jane thought it was a fly walking over her head when she felt the paint-brush in her sleep. 'Go away, fly,' she murmured, and that made Tom almost laugh out loud.

He slid down to the floor when he had finished. He wouldn't let the others go up and see what he had done, in case they wakened Amelia Jane. 'Wait till she wakes,' he said. 'Oh, won't it be funny at the party? We shan't need to introduce Amelia Jane to anyone! They'll only have to read what's on her forehead!'

Well, it *was* funny! The pixie guests came along in crowds, longing to dance to the music of the musical-box and to eat the little cakes that Dinah had cooked on the dolls'-house stove. The bear was the host, and he introduced everyone.

But he didn't need to say who Amelia Jane was because as soon as the guests saw her they all giggled and said: 'Oh, this is naughty Amelia Jane!'

Amelia Jane was surprised and cross. She didn't like being called naughty at a party. She frowned and sulked. But as soon as everyone came up to her, the same thing was said: 'Oh, this is naughty Amelia Jane!'

'Why do you say that?' said Amelia, crossly, and she frowned so

hard that she wrinkled up all the red
words on her forehead.

'Don't do that – we can't read
your name!' said a small pixie.
Amelia Jane stared at him.

'What do you mean, you can't
read my name? Of course you can't.
Don't be silly.'

'Oh, now I can,' said the little pixie, when Amelia had stopped frowning. 'Yes – this is naughty Amelia Jane.'

Amelia Jane went to the teddy bear, almost crying. 'Why is everyone horrid to me? Why do they keep saying, "This is naughty Amelia Jane"? Tell me.'

'No,' said the bear.

'Yes,' said Amelia. 'I want to know, please, please, bear.'

'I'll tell you if you promise to give me that red pencil and never to scribble anywhere again,' said the bear. 'It's a low thing to do.'

'All right,' said Amelia Jane, with a

sigh. 'I won't scribble any more. Here's the pencil.'

'Thanks. Now go and look at yourself in the mirror,' said the bear, and Amelia went.

She screamed when she saw the red words on her forehead. 'Oh! Oh, how mean! Now I know why everyone said what they did. I shan't go back to the party.'

So she didn't. She stayed and moped in the toy-cupboard, and that's where the bear found her halfway through. 'Come along,' he said. 'Come and dance.'

'No,' said Amelia. 'Not with this horrid scribble on my forehead.'

The bear took out his hanky. 'Lick it,' he said to Amelia Jane, and she licked his hanky. He rubbed the licky bit over her forehead.

'There!' he said. 'The scribble's gone. Now come along and dance – and mind you behave yourself, or I might write something else on you. You never know!'

So Amelia Jane behaved herself. But I'm afraid her good behaviour won't last long!

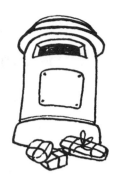

Amelia Jane Plays Postman

I really must tell you the latest story about Amelia Jane.

On the nursery mantelpiece stood a money-box. It looked exactly like a pillar-box, and it was painted red just like the big ones we post letters in down the road.

But instead of posting letters in

their box the children posted money, of course, and it was a very good way of saving it. 'Clink!' it went when it was dropped in, and the money-box grew heavier and heavier.

Mother kept the key of the box and only unlocked it when the children wanted to take out some money to buy someone a birthday present. She unlocked the box at the bottom then, and the children took the money out.

Now, Amelia Jane suddenly took it into her head that if she found anything left about by the toys she would post it in the red money-box on the mantelpiece! That made the toys very angry indeed.

'Amelia Jane! Have you taken my pink ribbon?' cried the bear.

'Yes. And I've posted it,' said Amelia. 'You are getting very untidy, Teddy, leaving your things about. It will teach you to be tidy.'

Teddy was furious, of course. And so was the clockwork clown when he found that Amelia had actually posted the button that came off his trousers.

'How dare you do that?' he shouted. 'I couldn't help it coming off, could I? I know somebody would have sewn it on again, if you hadn't picked it up and posted it. You're SILLY, Amelia Jane!'

And then she posted the toy soldier's belt! It was a bit tight, so he had undone it and had just put it down while he straightened his trousers a little, when Amelia Jane pounced on it. He was too late to get it back! Into the red money-box it went.

'Now I haven't got a belt!' shouted Tom. 'I look awful.

Stop this nonsense, Amelia Jane, or we'll start posting *your* things in that box!'

'You can't,' said Amelia with a grin. 'I'm the only one that can reach the mantelpiece.'

This was quite true. Amelia Jane was a very big doll and a good climber too. She could reach up to the chair near the fireplace, climb over to the mantelpiece and climb on to that. Then it was easy to post anything in the money-box there.

But none of the other toys could get on to the mantelpiece, so they couldn't possibly post anything belonging to Amelia. It was most annoying. After she had posted the baby doll's dear little comb, the toys held a meeting. Amelia Jane was asleep in her chair, so she didn't hear a word.

'We've got to do *some*thing to stop her,' said the clock. 'She'll be posting the clockwork mouse's tail next!'

The mouse gave a squeal. 'No, no! Don't say that! I couldn't bear it.'

'How can we stop her?' wondered the baby doll.

The teddy bear suddenly slapped his plump knee.

'I know. I've got an idea!'

'Sh! Don't wake Amelia,' said the clown.

'Now listen,' said the teddy, excitedly. 'You know next week it's the birthday of the little mouse who lives in the hole in the wall, don't you? Well, listen – ooooh, it's *such* a good idea – you see . . .'

'Oh, do go on! Do tell us!' said the clockwork mouse, impatiently.

'Well – we'll pretend that we are giving the little mouse all sorts of tiny presents, wrapped up in parcels,' said the teddy, grinning. '*But* – we'll put inside the parcels little things belonging to Amelia Jane! We'll put her best hair-ribbon in – and one of her Sunday shoes – and that brooch she likes so much – and her best sash . . .'

'But dear me, we can't *possibly* give her things to the little mouse,' said Tom, shocked. 'That would be quite wrong.'

'Oh, don't you *see* what will happen?' said the teddy. 'Amelia Jane will find the parcels – and she won't be able to stop herself *posting* them – in the money-box! And she'll have posted all her own things and won't be able to get them back!'

There was a silence. Then the toys giggled and thumped Teddy on the back. 'You're marvellous!' they cried. 'It is a simply wonderful idea! We'll do it! Oh, how we'll laugh to see Amelia posting her own things!'

 Well, they did just what they had planned. They found Amelia's brooch and wrapped it up. They found her best sash, folded it neatly and wrapped it in paper and tied it with string. They took her hair-ribbon and did that up too, and one of her best shoes! Soon there were four neat little parcels at the back of the toy-cupboard.

And, of course, it wasn't long before Amelia Jane found them. 'Aha!' she said. 'I suppose these are birthday parcels for that silly little mouse who lives in the wall. I'll post them!'

'I warn you not to,' said Tom. 'You'll be sorry if you do, Amelia.'

Amelia laughed and picked up all the parcels. She went towards the fireplace to climb on the chair there.

'You have been warned!' called the clown. But Amelia took no notice at all. Ha – this was a fine trick to play on the toys – to post all the parcels they had got ready for the little mouse!

Thud, thud, thud, thud! Down into the money-box they went, and there they stayed. Amelia Jane climbed down, smiling. 'I have been warned!' she said, mockingly. 'But *I* don't care.'

Nobody said anything. They just waited in patience till Amelia wanted her brooch or her ribbon or sash. She soon did, because she was to go to a party given by the doll in the next house. The children were taking her.

'I shall wear my best shoes, my sash, my blue hair-ribbon, and my brooch,' she said. 'I *shall* look grand!'

But she couldn't find them, though she hunted everywhere. She turned to the watching toys. 'You know something about them!' she cried. 'What have you done with them?'

'Nothing – except just wrap them up into neat little parcels!' grinned the clown.

'But what for? Oh, *what's* happened to my precious, precious things?' groaned Amelia.

'You should know,' said the bear. 'You picked up all the parcels yesterday.'

'You p-p-p-posted them!' squealed the clockwork mouse, stammering in excitement, and then going off into a fit of giggles.

'I *posted* them!' said Amelia. 'What do you mean? Those were birthday parcels for the mouse, weren't they? Oh, oh, oh – why didn't you tell me what they were?'

'We warned you, we did warn you not to post them,' said the clown, and

he went off into
giggles, too.

Amelia Jane cried
bitterly. She
didn't go to the
party. She
moped all
day long till
the toys felt quite sorry for her. Then
she dried her eyes.

'I'm sorry I posted everybody's
things,' she said. 'I know what it feels
like now to lose my things in that
money-box. I'll find the key, undo the
box and get everything out.'

But she couldn't find the key
because Mother had it in her purse.

So everything has got to stay there till somebody has a birthday and the money-box is unlocked.

And *what* a surprise the children are going to get when they see all the things that Amelia Jane has posted! I'm sure the clockwork mouse will have a fit of the giggles again!

Amelia Jane is Naughty Again

Listen to what Amelia Jane did a little while ago – she's almost as rascally as Brer Rabbit sometimes!

It all happened when a new toy came to stay in the nursery. He really belonged to the children's cousin, but she was going away and asked her cousins to look after this toy for her.

465

He was rather a peculiar-looking toy. He was made of wood, and he had jointed legs and arms and hands – and even toes. He was dressed like a gardener, with a green baize apron in front, a scarf round his neck, and rolled-up sleeves that showed his jointed arms.

The peculiar thing about him was his head. It could nod up and down and shake from side to side because it was on a kind of spring. It was very surprising to the toys to see somebody that could nod his head or shake it like that.

'What's your name?' asked Amelia Jane. 'Do we call you Mr Noddy or Mr Shaky?'

'I've got a cousin called Mr Shaky,' said the wooden man. 'I'm called Mr Up-and-To.'

'What a peculiar name!' said the sailor doll.

'Not really,' said the wooden man. 'Just a mixture of *Up*-and-Down and *To*-and-Fro – Mr Up-and-To.'

'Why not Mr Fro-and-Down?' asked Amelia Jane, and went off into giggles.

'How clever you are!' said Mr Up-

and-To, admiringly. 'That's a *much* nicer name! Really, I think you are a very clever doll.'

'Oh, I am,' said Amelia Jane at once. 'Aren't I, toys? If anything goes wrong, ask me how to put it right! If you want to know anything, ask me! If you –'

'That's enough, Amelia Jane,' said Tom. 'Stop blowing your own trumpet.'

'Oh, can she blow a trumpet, too?' said Mr Up-and-To, surprised. 'Well, well – if that isn't cleverer still. My mouth's too wooden to hold a trumpet.'

'Amelia's mouth is big enough to

hold a dozen trumpets, if she wanted to blow them about herself,' said the bear.

'Don't be unkind,' said Amelia Jane. 'You know I'm very clever.'

'I know you're very, very naughty,' said the bear. 'Now, you leave Mr Up-and-To alone, and don't stuff him up with any more tales.'

But Amelia Jane wouldn't leave the little wooden man alone. For one thing, he really was very, very stupid, and he believed every word anyone said. Amelia Jane found that out at once, and, oh, the tricks she played on that poor wooden man!

'Don't go near the brick-box,' she

would say. 'It's Monday today, and there might be a snake there!'

And, will you believe it, Mr Up-and-To would keep right the other side of the nursery, afraid that a snake might spring out at him.

'Don't go too near the Noah's Ark today, because it's Friday,' Amelia would say next. 'The lions are always so fierce on Friday.'

Mr Up-and-To didn't go near the Noah's Ark all day long. He asked Amelia Jane why the lions were so fierce on Fridays.

'Well, I expect that's the day they're fed at the Zoo,' said Amelia Jane, and the poor stupid little wooden man thought that was a very good reason.

'You're bad, Amelia Jane,' said Tom. 'Stuffing him up with tales like that. Whatever will you say next?'

'Aha! You wait and see!' said Amelia. And she went and whispered in Mr Up-and-To's big wooden ear.

'Don't go near the toy soldier today because it's Saturday and he might bite you.'

Poor Mr Up-and-To! He ran away as soon as Tom came near, and as Amelia Jane had given Tom a sweet to take to the wooden man, he kept on trying to find him, so that he could give him the sweet.

'I can't *think* why the wooden man keeps rushing off as soon as he sees me,' said Tom, surprised.

'It's Saturday and he doesn't like soldiers on Saturday,' said Amelia Jane, wickedly.

'Don't be silly,' said Tom. 'Here, take your sweet back. I'm not going

to rush after Mr Up-and-To all day long. You've told him something about me. I know you!'

Now one day Amelia Jane put a knot into her little blue hanky to remind her not to forget to mend her dress. Mr Up-and-To saw her knotting the knot, and he was most interested.

'What's that for?' he asked.

'Well, most people put a knot into their hanky if they want to remember something,' said Amelia. 'This knot says to me: "Mend your dress tonight, Amelia Jane." And I shall.'

'Very, very clever,' said the wooden man. 'I think I shall do that too,

Amelia. I'm always forgetting things, aren't I?'

'Well, you just try putting knots into your hanky, and you will soon have a marvellous memory,' said Amelia Jane.

So the next time Mr Up-and-To wanted to remember something, he took out his big, red-spotted hanky and tied a very large knot in it.

'That's to tell me to remember to clean my shoes tonight,' he said to himself. But, of course, when he saw the knot again he couldn't for the life of him remember what he had put it into his hanky for.

I'll ask Amelia Jane, he thought.

She always knows everything. So he went to find the big doll.

'Amelia,' he said, 'supposing I forgot what I had put a knot in my hanky for, would you be able to tell me?'

'Of course!' said Amelia, with a very wicked grin.

'Well, what's this knot for?' asked the wooden man, and he showed her the very big knot.

'Oh – that's to remind you to climb up to the basin-taps with a jug from the dolls' house, fill it with water, and give me a drink,' said Amelia at once.

'Is it really?' said the wooden man, in surprise. 'Well, fancy me forgetting that! I'll go at once, Amelia Jane.'

So, much to the toys' amazement, he got a jug, climbed all the way up to the basin, and held the jug under the tap-drips till he got it full. Then he gave Amelia Jane a drink.

'Well! He must be very fond of her,' said the clockwork clown, in surprise. 'Fancy doing all that for *Amelia*!'

Amelia was pleased. Her naughty mind began to work hard – and the very next time Mr Up-and-To was asleep she crept up to him, took his hanky from his pocket and made a very big knot there!

So, of course, the next time he took it out another knot stared him in the face. What *could* it be for?

'Oh, that?' said Amelia Jane. 'Dear, dear, have you forgotten already why you put it there, Mr Up-and-To? Why, it was to remind you to go to the toy sweet shop and bring me six of those tiny pink sweets.'

'Dear me – was it really?' said Mr Up-and-To, puzzled. 'I simply can't remember that at all! But I'll go at once, Amelia Jane.'

So he solemnly went to the toy-shop and took six of the little pink sweets from a bottle and gave them to Amelia Jane. She popped them all into her mouth at once.

Tom and the bear came over in a hurry. They spoke very sternly to Mr Up-and-To.

'Look here! That's stealing. Those sweets belong to the children, not to us. How dare you! Put them back!'

'He can't,' said Amelia, speaking with her mouth full. 'I'm eating them.'

'Did she tell you to get them?' the bear asked the wooden man.

'Well, no – not exactly. I – er – I put a knot in my hanky to remember to get them,' said Mr Up-and-To. 'I must say I'm very surprised at myself for putting a knot there to remind me of that. I'm very, very sorry, Teddy.'

Amelia Jane giggled to herself. She felt very naughty indeed, with a nice stupid fellow like Mr Up-and-To to play tricks on.

She put more knots in his hanky, and when he asked her what they could possibly be for she told him all sorts of things.

'That knot you put there is to remind you to get me the little blue brooch you'll find in a box at the back of the toy-cupboard,' she said. It belonged to the baby doll, and it was very bad of Amelia Jane to get the wooden man to fetch it for her.

'And that knot's to remind you to get me some cakes from the dolls'-house kitchen,' said Amelia another time. 'They've been baking today. And look, there's a little tiny knot in this corner of your hanky – that's to tell you to remember to have a cake for yourself, too.'

And, dear me, there were Amelia Jane and the wooden man both eating cakes together!

The toys were very, very angry, and the dolls'-house dolls threatened to fetch a policeman.

'If you tell Mr Up-and-To any more naughty things to do, we'll punish you, Amelia Jane,' said the bear. 'Oh, we know it's you all right! He's too stupid to think of these things himself. You put them into his head.'

Amelia got cross. She put *four* knots in Mr Up-and-To's hanky at once. He ran to her, most surprised, when he discovered them. 'Amelia Jane! Look here – I've put *four* knots this time. Whatever can they be for?'

'This one's to remind you to pull the toy soldier's nose, and this one's to remind you to tread on the tail of the clockwork mouse, and that's to tell you to be sure and pinch the teddy bear, and that's to remind you to run off with the clown's key,' said Amelia Jane.

Well, the wooden man was most astonished at himself. To think he had decided to do all those things and had actually put knots in his hanky to remind him. Well, well – he'd better start off with the toy soldier. He would pull his nose.

He tried to, but Tom caught his wooden hands, and stopped him.

'Listen, Mr Up-and-To,' he said sternly. 'What's up with you? You *seem*

so gentle and good, and a bit stupid –
and yet you do all kinds of very, very
naughty things. Why?'

'It's the knots in my hanky,'
explained the wooden man sadly.
'Amelia Jane always tells me what
they're for, you see. She knows.'

The toys went off to the back of
the toy-cupboard to have a meeting.
So *that's* what Amelia Jane was doing!

'She puts the knots in the hanky
when the old wooden man is asleep,'
said Teddy. 'And then when he asks
her what he's put them there for, she
tells him all kinds of nonsense. Well –
I'm going to tell him what his next
knot is for!'

The toys grinned. They could guess what the bear was going to tell Mr Up-and-To.

It was the bear that night who put a knot into the wooden man's hanky. It was such an enormous knot that the hanky seemed all knot when he had finished!

Mr Up-and-To was astonished to see such a big knot when he woke up. The bear was just nearby, so instead of asking Amelia Jane he showed the knot to Teddy.

'Look at that!' he said. 'A tremendous knot. Something *most* important to remember. I'd better ask Amelia Jane what it is for.'

'No, don't,' said the bear. 'She wouldn't dream of telling you what the knot's for. Ask me – or the toy soldier – or the clown. We all know. We'll tell you all right.'

'Tell me then,' said the wooden man.

'That knot, that very large knot, is to remind you to be sure and give Amelia Jane a good scolding,' said the bear. 'Don't look so surprised. That's what the knot is there for. Isn't it, Tom? Isn't it, everyone?'

And all the toys nodded and said yes, that was what the very large knot meant.

'She's been bad to you,' said

Teddy. 'She's tried to make you bad, too. She must be punished – and you are the one to punish her, Mr Up-and-To. Go now.'

So he's gone to find Amelia Jane, feeling very cross indeed. She tried to make him bad, did she? Mr Up-and-To didn't want to be bad. He'd give Amelia Jane a good scolding!

She's hiding, of course. But the wooden man will find her. He's very, very determined once he makes his mind up – and sooner or later there'll be howls from the nursery, I'm sure of that.

I don't feel a bit sorry, and neither does anyone else. Amelia Jane has had her fun, and now, alas, she's got to pay for it!

Amelia Jane Goes Up the Tree

It was springtime, and the birds were all nesting. Amelia Jane was most excited.

'The birds are building their nests,' she said. 'They are laying eggs.'

'Well, they do that every year,' said Tom.

'I want to make a collection of

birds' eggs,' said Amelia Jane, grandly.

'You naughty doll!' said the clockwork clown. 'You know quite well you mustn't take birds' eggs.'

'Well, I don't see why birds can't spare me one or two of their eggs,' said Amelia. 'After all – they can't count.'

'Amelia Jane, you know quite well that birds get dreadfully upset if they see anyone near their nests,' said the teddy bear. 'You know that sometimes they get very frightened, and they desert their nests – leave them altogether – so that the eggs get cold, and never hatch out.'

'Oh, don't lecture me so!' said Amelia Jane. 'I said I wanted to make a collection of birds' eggs, and so I am going to. You can't stop me.'

'You are a very bad doll,' said the clown, and he turned his back on Amelia. 'I don't like you one bit.'

Amelia Jane laughed. She was feeling in a very naughty mood. She looked out of the window, down into a big chestnut tree. In the fork of a branch was a nest. It belonged to a thrush.

'There's a thrush's nest just down there,' said Amelia. 'I wish I could climb down. But I can't. It's too dangerous. Perhaps I could climb up.'

'How could you do that?' said the curly-haired doll, in a scornful voice. 'Don't be silly. None of us could climb up that tall trunk!'

But the next day Amelia Jane was excited. 'The gardener has put a ladder up the chestnut tree!' she said. 'He has, really. He is cutting off some of the bigger branches, because they knock against the low roof of the shed. I shall slip down, wait till the gardener has gone to his dinner, and then climb the ladder!'

'Amelia Jane! You don't mean to say you really *are* going to rob a bird's nest!' cried the clown.

'Oh yes,' said Amelia. 'Why

should the bird mind if one or two eggs are taken? She will probably be glad that she hasn't so many hungry beaks to fill, when the eggs hatch out!'

So, to the horror of the watching toys, Amelia Jane slipped downstairs, out of the garden door and up to the ladder, as soon as the gardener had gone to his dinner.

The toys all pressed their noses to the window and watched her.

'She's climbing the ladder!' said the clown. 'She really is!'

'She's up to the top of it!' squeaked the clockwork mouse.

'She's going right into the tree!' cried the teddy bear, and he almost broke the window with his nose, he pressed so hard against it.

Amelia Jane was climbing the tree very well. She was a big strong doll, and she swung herself up easily. She soon came to the big thrush's nest. The mother-thrush was not there.

I suppose she has gone to stretch her wings a little, thought Amelia Jane. She stretched out her hand and put it into the nest. There were four eggs there,

and they felt smooth and warm.
Amelia Jane took one and put it into
the pocket of her red dress. Then she
took another, and put that in her
second pocket.

'There!' she said. 'Two will be
enough, I think. I can start a very nice
collection with two. How pretty they
are! I like them.'

She sat up in the tree for a little
while, enjoying the sound of the wind
in the leaves and liking the swaying of
the bough she sat on. It was so
exciting.

'I'd better go back now,' she said.
'I don't want to be here when the
mother-thrush comes back.'

So she began to climb
down the tree again.
But, after a while, she
heard a noise. It was
someone whistling.
She peeped down
between the
leaves.

'It's the
gardener!'
said Amelia
Jane in dismay.

'Oh dear, I hope he isn't coming up the tree now.'

He wasn't. He was doing something else – something that filled Amelia Jane with great dismay.

'He's taking away the ladder! Oh my! It's gone! However am I to get down again? The ladder's gone!'

It certainly *was* gone. The gardener, still whistling, carried it away for another job. And there was Amelia Jane, left high up the tree!

She sat there for a long time. She heard the thrush come back again to her nest. She heard the wind in the trees. She saw the toys in the nursery looking out at her in surprise, wondering why she didn't climb down and come back.

'I do feel lonely and frightened,' said Amelia to herself, when the day went and the cold night began to come. 'I shall be very afraid up here in the dark. Oh dear, why ever did I think of climbing the tree and stealing eggs? It's a punishment for me, it really is!'

She began to cry. And when Amelia Jane cried she made a noise. She sobbed and gulped and howled. It was a dreadful noise.

A small pixie, who lived in the primrose bed below, heard the noise and wondered what it was. So she flew up into the tree to see.

'Oh, it's you, Amelia Jane,' said the pixie. 'What's the matter? You're keeping me awake with that dreadful noise.'

'I can't get down,' sobbed Amelia. 'I want to get back to the nursery, and I can't.'

'Whatever made you climb up?' asked the pixie. But Amelia was too ashamed to tell her.

'Please help me,' begged the big doll. 'I am so unhappy.'

'Well, maybe the thrush who lives higher up the tree can help you,' said the pixie, and she flew up to see. Amelia Jane felt most uncomfortable.

She had taken eggs from the thrush's nest. Oh dear! How she wished she hadn't!

The pixie flew back again, and the big brown thrush was with her.

'Here's the thrush,' said the pixie. 'She is very sad and unhappy tonight, because some horrid person stole two of her precious eggs, but she is very kind, and although she is sad she will help you.'

'Yes, I will help you, help you, help you,' sang the thrush sweetly. 'I am

sad, sad, sad, but I will help you, big, big doll.'

'How can you help me?' asked Amelia in surprise.

'I can guide you right up the tree,' said the thrush. 'I know the way. I can bring you right up to the nursery window-sill, and you can knock on the window and get the toys to let you in. Then you will be safe, safe, safe!'

'Oh, you *are* kind!' said Amelia Jane. She turned to follow the thrush up the tree.

'Hold on to one of my tail-feathers,' said the thrush kindly. 'Don't be afraid of pulling it out.'

Amelia held on to a feather, and

the thrush guided her gently up the dark tree. After a little while she stopped and spoke.

'Big doll, can you see my nest just here? It is such a nice, comfortable one. It is very dark now, but perhaps you can just see two eggs gleaming in the cup. Aren't they lovely?'

Amelia Jane could see them gleaming in the half-darkness. The thrush went on, half speaking, half singing.

'You know, I had more eggs than those you see. But whilst I was away this morning someone took two, took two, took two. It nearly broke my heart. Now I shall only have two children instead of four. Can you imagine anyone bad enough to steal from a little bird like me?'

Amelia Jane felt the two eggs in her pockets, and she began to sob. 'What's the matter?' asked the kindly thrush; and she pressed her warm, feathery body close to Amelia to comfort her.

'Oh, brown thrush, oh, brown thrush,' sobbed Amelia. 'I took your eggs. I've got them in my pockets. Let me put them back into your nest, please, please! They are still lovely and warm, and I haven't broken them. I'm the horrid person that took them, but I'm dreadfully sorry now!'

She took the warm eggs from her pockets and put them gently into the nest.

'Now push me down the tree; do anything you like to punish me!' said Amelia Jane. 'I know I deserve it.'

'What a foolish doll you are!' said the thrush, very happy to see her eggs once more. 'Because you were unkind to me is no reason why I should now be unkind to you. I am happy again, so I want to make you happy, too! Come along, hold on to my tail-feather, and we'll go higher till we come to the window-sill!'

So up they went, with Amelia wiping her eyes on her skirt every now and again because she was so ashamed of herself and so grateful to the thrush for forgiving her and being kind to her.

They came to the window-sill, and Amelia rapped on it. The teddy bear, who was just the other side, called the clown, and together they opened the window. Amelia slipped inside. She said goodbye to the thrush, and then looked at the toys.

'Whatever happened to you?' said the clown. 'Did you take the eggs? Surely that was the thrush helping you just now!'

'I did take the eggs, but I've given them back, and I'm ashamed of myself for taking them,' said Amelia in a very small voice. 'I shall never, never do such a thing again in my life. I'm going to be a Good Doll now.'

'Hmmm,' said the clown. 'We've

heard that before, Amelia Jane! We'll see what the thrush has to say tomorrow!'

I heard her singing the next day, and do you know what she sang? She sang: 'Took two, took two, put them back, put them back, put them back, sweet, sweet, sweet!' Listen, and maybe you'll hear her singing that, too!

Enid Blyton

THE
FARAWAY
TREE
COLLECTION

THREE EXCITING STORIES IN ONE!

Enid Blyton

The Faraway Tree
Collection

The Enchanted Wood
The Magic Faraway Tree
The Folk of the Faraway Tree

Join Jo, Bessie and Fanny on their adventures
in the Enchanted Wood, where the children visit
the Land of Birthdays, the Land of Topsy-Turvy
and other amazing places at the top of
the Faraway Tree.

Enid Blyton

THE
MYSTERIES
COLLECTION

THREE EXCITING STORIES IN ONE!

Enid Blyton

The
Mysteries
Collection

The Mystery of the Spiteful Letters
The Mystery of the Missing Necklace
The Mystery of the Hidden House

In these three adventures, the irrepressible
Five Find-Outers – Larry, Daisy, Pip, Bets
and Fatty, plus Buster the dog – solve three
exciting mysteries, in spite of the efforts
of PC Goon to stop them . . .